THE SWEETEST THINGS

STARLIGHT HARBOR #1

BRIA QUINLAN

ALSO BY BRIA QUINLAN

BREW HA HA Series

It's In His Kiss (FREE Prequel)

The Last Single Girl

Worth the Fall

The Catching Kind

The Proposing Kind

Things That Shine - A Crossover Brew Ha Ha /Double Blind Story

Bria's YA set RVHS Secrets

Secret Girlfriend

Secret Life

And YA Standalone

Wreckless

1

Lyra

"THAT MAN." LYRA GRIGOR SLAMMED HER TINY, FLOUR covered fist down on the counter. "That...words, words, words man."

Her best friend, Vivian, looked up from where she was sipping her coffee and eating an old-fashioned donut. "Must be pretty bad to have gotten the triple words curse replacement."

Lyra glanced past her to make sure the bakery was empty. She didn't want people to think the owner of The Sweetest Things had suddenly become a crazy web stalker. But this article on the travel blog *Roadside Adventures* was really bringing out a thread of *ticked off* in her she wasn't used to.

She was used to being the softhearted mushy one.

"Well, you're in here this year, too. Made the cut, so to say." She glanced down at the tablet and read, "...so quaint it even has a female mechanic for the four cars in town."

"Huh." Vi took another bite of her donut—well, her second donut—and sat back on her barstool, knowing Lyra didn't let things go easily that riled her up.

Lyra glared at the so-called article: "Top Ten Tacky Tiny Towns."

It just beat her butter that there was even an article, let alone that Starlight Harbor, with its gorgeous port and its wonderful traditions, made the list.

There was nothing tacky about what they did here.

Four years running they'd been on his insulting list.

"I bet he hasn't even been here. He just heard about our Christmas schedule, turned that into 'Christmas every day,' and puts us up there with the largest ball of twine or the singing shark."

That got Vi's attention. "Where's the singing shark?"

"Yeah. It got taken off in year two because it was proven to be a hoax." She flashed Vivian a triumphant look. "See? This guy can't even research articles enough to spot a fraud."

"Well, there ya go." Vivian glanced at the pastry case, considering.

"You know," Lyra jumped in, "if I didn't love you, I'd totally hate you. I see you eyeing that cookie after two donuts."

She gave her friend the once-over. Vivian's tall, thin frame could probably carry a couple more pounds and not look out of place. But she carried her model body and looks and hair with something close to disdain, the tough chick keeping all her worries locked out with her kickass boots and her fitted tanks.

Granted, that was also what she needed to wear to work in her garage, but still. Vivian didn't take crap. She'd come back to town with her son and lived on her own terms since.

Vivian wouldn't let someone kick around people she loved.

"You know what?" Lyra demanded, getting Vi's attention from the sugar in the glass case between them. "I'm not letting him get away with this again. I stood by for three years thinking he'd let it go. But, every year he finds tackier and tackier things that are just roadside tourist rip-offs but keeps Starlight Harbor on there."

Lyra grabbed her tablet, setting up an account with the stupid wannabe travel magazine site.

"Someone needs to give this bully a piece of her mind."

Vi set her coffee cup on the bus tray, grinning indulgently as she stuffed a dollar in the tip jar that kept appearing on Lyra's counter no matter how many times she took it away.

"Go get him, tiger."

"Yeah, yeah." She waved Vi off, because she was already typing madly into the comments section.

Dear Mr. Judger of People's Homes,

I can't help but notice that for a fourth year in a row you've included Starlight Harbor, Maine, on your list of Tiny Tacky Towns. The only tacky thing here is taking a beautiful community who honors military families by creating a place to celebrate the holidays they were separated for based while serving ungrateful ~~jackasses~~ bullies.

While you may not appreciate these traditions, I would think that at least the sheer beauty of the Maine coast and a centuries-old village would be obvious even to a Neanderthal like you.

Perhaps you didn't do your research, or you just hate Christmas. I mean, we all know that sharks can't sing.

Well, *most* of us do.

Next time, before you attack hardworking people and their quaint seaside village, you should do your research. Perhaps start with the definition of the word *tacky*. I've included a link to the word's page in Merriam-Webster.

That's a dictionary, for those who don't know. It tells you what words mean.

Yours,
Starlight Cupcake

Lyra stared at her words and got angry all over again. How dare he attack a place where people were dedicated to helping others?

He obviously had no soul.

Thank goodness she didn't have to deal with people like that. It was the number one reason she'd had no doubt she'd come back to Starlight Harbor after she finished getting her degree from Johnson & Wales.

She'd seen what the competition and the general ambitions of the city had done to her fellow pastry chefs and bakers. The push to get ahead had quickly made the beauty of baking and the joy it gave others shrink in importance.

But now, now that she'd said her piece, all was right in her world again—and she had cookies to decorate for the Historical Society's trip to the hospital to tell stories about smugglers and their mascot dogs to the children.

Life was pretty darn good.

Spence

SPENCE CÔTE'S LIFE WAS A MESS. AN ABSOLUTE MESS.

Classic case of if he knew then what he knew now.

Pulling up his month's numbers, he tallied his ad revenue for *Roadside Adventures* and knew this was the closest to fixing his life he'd been in years. He was so close he could almost see the tipping point within reach.

It had seemed like such a good idea when he'd started the site. Just a stupid hobby while he was looking for a job after college.

He'd had too much time and energy to burn—which, at thirty wasn't as much of a problem as it had been at twenty-two. And after driving back across the country, all his belongings in his old, beat-up clunker, he'd seen so many crazy things he'd wanted to share them.

It had started out as funny. *Hey! Check this out! Can you believe there's actually an entire museum of fake dinosaur bones rejected by paleontologists?* Who wouldn't want to stop and take a driving break to see that?

It was supposed to let him get in some fun writing while he searched for that perfect journalism job. The one he didn't get right out of college because he'd been stupid and done the summer between junior and senior year in Southeast Asia with his girlfriend instead.

Now, the older he got, the more it wore on him. He tried to deviate to funny, inspiring articles about his travels through Europe and Asia. To share with his readers more earnest and honest experiences that showed the beauty of our world. They did okay, but not like his top ten lists or snarkier pieces. People used those to create road trips. His site was added again and again to the must-have lists for road trip planning.

He'd created a template for the year at this point—small towns, amusement parks, craziest historical markers, weirdest junkyards...the list of lists went on.

People loved this stuff.

He got hundreds of photos a week uploaded to his directory now.

And ad clicks that paid the bills.

What had started as a hobby while he chased being a travel writer had slowly taken over his life. He could barely remember the last trip where he was able to unplug for more than two days.

There was no way to write a travel exposé in two days.

Every day, every moment he worked on *Roadside Adventures*, he felt his dreams slipping away.

But, at the same time, he'd built a large enough following —and he'd spent the money he earned as it came in— creating his own financial prison.

Because he was apparently stupid.

His own coffee table was littered with copies of *National Geographic* and *The Smithsonian* and other amazing, deeply crafted collections.

All the places he longed to write for—all the articles he wished he'd written.

At least *Roadside Adventures* was low maintenance in its dealing with trolls and such. The conversations were usually more humorous than not, even people chiming in that they'd been to the location and their thoughts or some suggestions on what else could have been included.

On the flip side, he'd just seen an amazing article on the destruction of Middle Eastern artifacts as acts of war—especially in Syria—and after he'd read it, he expected the comments to reflect his own feelings: that of unjust loss for the beauty and gifts from the past.

Instead, it was riddled with hate and anger and doubt that it had even happened, or that if it had "they" deserved it.

The fact that people didn't understand that art belonged to all of us—no matter the culture that created it—confused him beyond belief.

Roadside Adventures' commenters could perhaps be mocking in tone, but they weren't cruel. But, he did have to moderate them for spam and the occasional argument about the order of his lists. People felt really strongly about which waterpark was the best in the midwest or which chili dog should be rated the number one must try.

He opened the day's posts and sat back in shock. He had to have gotten hit by a spambot, but geez. 751 comments since eight this morning? That was a record for sure.

The most he'd ever had was like seventy when he'd done a post on churches that were now homes. It had taken nearly a week to get that many and it was because people were fascinated by the buildings *and* because there was an argument about damnation based on religion.

He'd shut that down.

No politics, no religion. He was a travel site. He wasn't qualified to moderate those topics.

Since all of the comments seemed to be on his Tiny Towns article, he might as well clean that out first. There

7

were two posts he had to write for tomorrow still and he wasn't feeling either of them.

Which was par for the course lately.

The first two comments were typical—expressing thanks for more crazy roadside stops. It was the third that brought him up short, and the reply number was insane. He clicked to open it all the way, doubting this was going to make his day go any smoother.

Dear Mr. Judger of People's Homes...

3

Lyra

IT TOOK FOUR ORDERS BEFORE LYRA CAUGHT ON.

She was going to blame her eternal optimism for that and chalk it up to being a happy person. As a little girl, she'd realized that there were two paths when your mom was off on adventures and your dad had left for good: keep it happy or not-so-happy.

So, happy it was.

Most of the time.

When the phone rang again, she'd had enough of a break between it and the last phone call to realize something was going on. That was the thing about the food industry. Sometimes you didn't get time to stop and breathe—or think.

But, after a few sips of tea, she knew a storm of craziness was truly hitting her that shouldn't.

"The Sweetest Things. How can I help you?"

"Yes, I'd like to order four hundred cupcakes for an event next weekend. The theme is tacky toppings."

Lyra rolled her eyes. She was on to the game now that it had dawned on her exactly what was going on. If she hadn't been, this guy would have blown all the prankers' covers with that super-obvious remark.

"Right. That's a great theme. I'm sure we can handle your order. It's just...well, George Clooney is doing his annual— oh. I mean, we're booked solid for... um, things. You know, we're just a small town bakery and no one remotely interesting ever comes to the coast of Maine."

She paused, as if waiting for a response, before rushing on.

"But, if you're local, I'd suggest going up to Portland. They have some bakeries almost as good as ours. I studied with one at Johnson & Wales and can tell you that while his buttercream frosting is superb, he does use a bit of a light hand with it."

She waited this time, silence on the end.

"Was there anything else I can do for you?"

"Um...no?"

"I didn't think so." She hung the phone up with such force she was shocked the glass screen didn't crack.

Now that she knew who was to blame, she was so going to take care of this.

Just after she handled what were potentially three false orders before she put her weekly order in.

"Hi, this is Lyra confirming your company's order for next week. No? You aren't a company, and you didn't order anything? Sorry to bother you."

And so it went, through all three phone numbers. Although, one person got on her site, declared it "delightful," and promised to give them a call if they ever did anything like her Decedent Desserts party again.

She put the phone on mute and went back to work, mulling just how angry she was.

The fact that this could have cost her, a small business, owned and run by one person, six figures in wasted food and energy was enough for her to say yes. She was very, very angry.

Pulling up the article again, she scanned through the replies to her comment. Hundreds of them. It was very, very clear the type of people who enjoyed a site dedicated to mocking other people's happy spots.

After treating herself to a lemon cookie something she almost never did—she sat down and pounded out a response.

To the owner of this site and the commenters who attacked my business,

I'm not sure why you would do this or even how much energy it took, but I've spent the day trying to figure out what calls are real—and not letting those customers down—and those that are fake. The fake ones could have cost me over a hundred-thousand dollars, perhaps bankrupting me.

And yet, I doubt anyone here cares about that.

The tone of not only the articles but the comments led me to believe that trying to point out that this lovely part of a beautiful state doesn't deserve four years of mockery.

I guess that was asking too much.

Please call your army off, or I'll send mine your way. Mine would be the town lawyer.

Sincerely,

Starlight Cupcake

Lyra read it over. Her tone was stronger than usual but far less forward than her angry WWVD—which, next time she decided to go with What Would Vivian Do, she needed to stop herself immediately.

She'd said her piece.

And, honestly, even if it cost her a little trouble in the short run, she was glad she'd done it. It was over, and—

"What is going on with you?"

Her mother burst into her bakery, her standard brightly dyed linen scarves over her equally bright flowing sundress, a rush of color and energy.

"What do you mean?"

"My Google alerts are going crazy. I thought it was your brother at first. Sometimes I think I need to stop following him. Really, there's only so much a mother should know about her son's sex life—even as free-spirited as I believe my liberal soul to be—"

"Mom." Lyra glanced toward the sky, wondering if help was coming. "What's with the Google alerts emergency? Is something going on with Rion?"

"At first I thought you got another write-up about the wonderful cake you did for the Taste of Maine event, but then it was just…oh, honey."

Her mother was giving her the *someone died* look. Which she never actually used when someone died, so Lyra wasn't overly worried.

Her mother enjoyed drama. Or, as she'd put it, the excitement of a shifting chi fed her soul.

So yeah…worry, schmorry.

"Your Yelp page rating is down to a 1.4."

Lyra shook her head. "That can't be right. It was nearly a five-star rating with over sixty reviews last time I looked. That was like three weeks ago when I checked the summer hours were correct."

"Well, honey. You must have ticked off a New Kid on the Block or something."

"Mom, they're…okay, never mind. I get your point. But, really. It must be a glitch. It happens. There's no way it could have dropped like that. It would take—"

Lyra froze midsentence, the horrible comments from that horrible site flashing through her mind again. Turning away from her mom without a word, she hurried back to her tablet, already knowing what she'd find. And yes, her mom and Google alerts were right. Her Yelp page had been attacked.

It wouldn't be such a bad thing—well, it would be, but not *horrible*—if the town and the state travel sites didn't use the Yelp ratings and top reviews as their listings.

Anyone who visited Starlight Harbor while it was being attacked would get the Yelp rating...on Yelp, the town, the state, and the top travel site.

Basically, it was like the atomic bomb of review attacks.

She put in a report for abuse and stared at the screen, watching the 1.4 drop to a 1.3 as she did.

Opening up the Evil Article again, she typed in a demand—no! A challenge.

Hey, Mob Boss,
　　Call me.
　　Starlight Cupcake

.

4

Spence

MOB BOSS?

Spence was pretty sure that whatever was happening on his website was not the full extent of what ticked off the cupcake grandmother.

He should have just closed this down instead of reading all the comments live. Grandma Cupcake got doxxed, and who knows what else people were doing—obviously creating false orders, which, he was sure, his people thought was just a prank.

But, she had a point. What if she bought all that food, hired help, and created huge orders for these catered affairs people were claiming they had?

He wasn't sure what he'd find if he kept digging, but the words *mob boss* didn't make him confident that was all of it.

If it got out that his site went after some innocent old grandmother who sold cupcakes in some tiny little back-water Maine town, he'd be destroyed. He'd never get out of debt, let alone sell his site for enough that he could focus on a real career as a travel reporter.

The only offerings he'd get were from people with no

scruples looking to create post-Reddit world sites where doxxing was standard and clickbait ad-heavy slideshow reads were the norm.

While he wasn't exactly a crusader himself, he'd hate that something he created became a weapon to hurt people.

Pulling up her company's website, he was relieved to see that at least she hadn't been hacked. He put a Google alert on her company name. If anything went awry, he'd know as soon as Google knew. He couldn't keep checking… Next up was her Yelp page, but that should be—

Holy crap.

He'd seen all the reviews along the side of her website and they were amazing. He doubted that she'd been able to get any of those if she really was a 0.7 rating on Yelp.

No wonder she threatened to find a lawyer.

Okay, so a town lawyer. What the heck was a town lawyer?

No matter how backwoods this lawyer was, he couldn't afford any fight—even if it was some My Cousin Vinny Northern New England type thing.

At least he had a contact at Yelp. It was going to just about kill him to admit this was his readership's doing, but he had to get in front of this mess as soon as possible. He'd just sent financials to both the companies who had expressed interest in buying him out, and he had a feeling that a phone call was not going to fix it.

There was only one option.

Spence glanced at the clock and pulled up his phone's GPS.

It was going to be a long night.

5

Lyra

LYRA TURNED OFF HER PHONE AND WEBSITE. THAT SEEMED TO be the only way she was going to manage taking care of her regulars and getting ready for the next Holidayer weekend.

Of course, she'd swung back to her WWVD focus when she'd seen her Yelp page. If that guy—Spence Côte—wanted to declare war?

All right, then, she'd declare war.

She had already put a phone call in to the person who could most help her fix this before she'd opened that morning.

Not to be a cliché or anything, but her big brother could fix anything. And if he couldn't, her sister knew people.

Okay, okay. Her sister denied constantly that she was CIA, but she sure did travel to places where she was "unavailable" a lot, so Lyra was going with spook.

And, of course, neither of them were available. Rion's manager said he'd get back to her. Her sister's number just went straight to voicemail.

That wasn't suspicious.

She was thinking about locking up since the post-camp

kid stream had finished, when the bell over the door rang and Vivian strode in with their friend Skye, the deputy sheriff.

"Your mother came by." Skye grinned.

Right. Her mom.

"Whose rear needs to meet my boot?" Skye went on in her typical no-nonsense cop voice.

"I'm so sorry. My mom seems to think you can do anything."

"Please. It's totally okay." Skye snorted. "I mean, I *can* do anything as far as your mom is concerned. But, no. I can't drive to whatever basement this guy is working out of and —and I quote—drag him by the ear back here to jail and keep him there until he apologizes like a gentleman and whole spirit would. She also said he must be a Leo or a Sagittarius."

"Of course." Lyra snorted as she headed toward the door and threw the lock, flipping the open sign to closed in one practiced move.

Skye dropped down at their table and pulled out a piece of paper with a bunch of notes on it.

"I can't arrest anyone. But I did get his IP address location from the domain his site is listed under. Also, I put in a call to a friend who knows everyone."

"Awwww…" Vivian gave her an overly-awed look. "You mean, you called Dev down in Boston and asked him what all that meant and he just did it?"

"Hey, I got it done, right? Now we know that Spence Côte lives in New York—Upstate, not city—and we can check out the harassment laws specifically for there and here."

Vivian gave her an agreeable nod.

"Guys. I may have posted again telling him to call me. There may have been name-calling involved." Lyra was a little worried she'd overstepped the line there.

17

Vi looked fascinated by this idea. She all but rubbed her hands together. "What did you call him?"

"Well, I started with jackass…"

"No," they both shouted at Lyra as Vivian crossed around the counter to take out a red velvet cupcake and a blonde brownie bar and poured three cups of tea as Lyra paced the shop from front to back. While her friend wasn't looking, Vi slipped ten bucks in the tip jar, because, yes. Besties still paid for food.

"I deleted it." She looked a little disappointed in herself at that. "But! I did tell him he was a bully. And then after everything went nuts, I called him a mob boss."

Skye snorted tea out her nose.

"Really? That was your go-to biggest insult?"

"Well, he was getting his people to create all this havoc to try to bring me down. So, mob boss." She bit into Vivian's red velvet cake, enjoyed a second burst of sugar for the day, then handed it back. "And then the article disappeared."

"Wow, you must have really ticked him off to get him to lock down his site." Skye made some notes in her little cop notebook.

Vivian once accused her of doodling just to look important. Skye was so incensed she'd held the notebook up and flipped pages to prove there were no doodles. Of course, she did that from three feet away because of confidentiality issues. She wanted to make sure she did it by the book.

Lyra wasn't sure there was a code in "the book" about disproving doodle rumors, but okay.

She was just glad they were getting along, doodles notwithstanding.

Those two had had a rough start when Vi came back to town. Things smoothed out quickly when Skye saw that Vivian wasn't going to be the troublemaker her reputation shouted she was. Vi was okay with Skye when she saw she wasn't out to get her. Now the doodle comment would be a joke, not a dig.

"Maybe." Lyra glanced down at her tablet, wondering if the comments would ever come back up. "But he could have responded. I mean, I put my email there and my website in that little form."

They both stared at her for a long minute before Skye lowered her head to the table and slowly beat it against the wood.

"I don't suppose you put your home address, cell number, and social security digits, too?"

"Of course not!"

Skye got up and headed toward the door. "Be right back. Work stuff. Just have to check in."

She was already reaching for the walkie clipped to her shoulder as the door fell shut behind her.

Vivian stared at Lyra with a serious look Lyra wasn't sure what to do with.

"I screwed up with the whole no-one-knows-you-on-the-internet thing, right?"

Vi gave her head a slight nod, obviously biting her tongue.

"But the boxes said they wouldn't be shown to anyone. I thought that meant that no one would see them except that guy who—" Lyra stopped, a blush of red rushing up her cheeks, making her strawberry-blonde hair stand out even more. "You know when you're so angry, like ticked-off angry, and you just don't think straight and then you don't even realize you weren't thinking straight until much later when —as my mom would put it—the chickens are coming home to roost."

"Oh, honey." Vivian reached out and took her hand across the table. "You just described like half of my life."

"No. You grew up fast, but look how good you're doing."

"Lyra, you stood by me before. And you even kept in touch when I was gone. But...I was too ashamed to let you know every stupid thing I was doing. Trust me. Not thinking straight and putting your email address somewhere is small potatoes. You're going to have to work harder to catch up with me in the screw-up hierarchy."

She gave Lyra's hand a quick squeeze as the front door opened and Skye came back in and threw the lock again.

"Sorry about that. Forgot to check in."

"Or you alerted all your little deputy people that I basically told my new arch enemy where I lived and to make sure that his minions didn't just show up at my house and harass me?"

"Yes." Skye gave her a quick grin. "Or that."

"What would I do without you guys?" Lyra reached out for both her friends' hands and gave them a squeeze. "This adulting thing is really hard."

Vivian snorted and pushed out of her chair. "Try it with a kid."

"Come on. Let's get some real food and maybe one of those adult beverages." Skye tucked her chair in and waited for Lyra to grab her bag.

"Finally! An adulting upside!"

6

Spence

THIS WAS NOT WHAT HE EXPECTED. ABSOLUTELY NOTHING LIKE he could have even pictured.

Where were the inflatable Santas and the piped-in Christmas carols? The fake snow and the tourist-herders dressed as elves? The streets had signs like Main and Water. The stores missed out, too. Not one The Book Elf or Jolly Baker puns.

The only pun he could see was Ms. Cupcake's shop—The Sweetest Things—and that was a normal bakery pun. No bad Christmas wording involved at all.

Even the decorations were mild and tasteful.

He looked closely as he drove through, spotting where things were tucked away and assuming they came out for events.

So, it wasn't Christmas *every* day?

He was surprised how few pictures of the town were online. The town itself didn't do much in terms of advertising its Christmas thing. How did anyone stay in business like this?

Couldn't these people see he was doing them a favor? All it got him was attacked on his own site.

He shook his head, completely off mission after driving through the night to handle the cupcake lady himself.

Slowing down, he let the traffic jam subside—a mama duck and her little squad of ducklings following along behind her.

He was annoyed by how charming that was.

He was not here to be charmed. He was here to make sure he wasn't getting sued, fix any damage that had been done, and try to make peace with the outspoken baker.

He didn't even have any posts for today. He put up an old flashback favorite—a first time he'd ever done that except the time his brother had been in the hospital—and turned the comments off.

Yeah. He did that.

And so of course his Twitter feed had blown up with people commenting about the lack of comments.

But, low priority.

He turned onto the small square, the GPS telling him to follow around the far edge and that his destination would be on the right.

Instead of parking immediately, he did a loop, drove down to the water then back up, and went over to the inn pictured on that town's website and around. Basically got a vibe for what the town was like and...stalled.

Yup. He was stalling.

Maybe he should have brought the little baker flowers as a peace offering or something.

Instead, he sucked it up and parked in front of the shop two doors down from The Sweetest Things.

Putting the car into park, he noticed the third cop car he'd seen. Did they have high crime here or something? Or maybe a quick visit from a local celebrity. Kennebunkport,

Castle Rock, Camden…all popular places for famous people with lots of money…or, you know, presidents.

Hopping out of the third-hand Corolla, Spence swung his messenger bag over his shoulder and headed over. There was a small, tiny hope in his heart that this drive was a waste of time. That he'd be in and out with everything solved, and maybe a box of pastries for his mom.

His gut was not as hopeful.

Pushing into the bakery, he switched his sunglasses for his actual lenses. It was cooler than he expected with its east-facing picture windows and huge ovens. Comfortable. He was betting no matter what it was like outside, it was always comfortable in here.

Grandmothers typically had that ability, though. Like a Nana Superpower or something.

Little tables were scattered around the room, each with a couple of surprisingly cozy-looking chairs, as if the owner wasn't going to rush you out the door just because you took your last bite of that delicious-looking cake in the pastry display.

How many layers did that thing have? Eight? Nine?

He honed in on it, nearly dropping to his knees to get a look at its gooey perfection.

"That's a triple chocolate with raspberry layer cake."

"No." Spence took his phone out and shot a couple pictures from a few different angles. "It's a work of art."

He was about to say he'd feature it in an article if it tasted as good as it looked, then remembered why he was there.

Probably not the way to start this conversation.

He straightened, rising past the cakes, then the cupcakes, then cookies, right up past the counter display to… the most beautiful thing in the shop.

"Oh. Hi." He glanced around, afraid he was about to make an ass of himself in front of the pale-haired angel.

She was all of five-four, with tiny freckles dancing across her pale, pert nose and the fairest strawberry-blonde hair he'd ever seen. She wore a dress with straps showing off the baker's strength of her arms and attractive swish to her skirt.

"Hi." She flashed him a smile. "Can I help you?"

"Oh. Yeah. Hey." Spence glanced around, trying to figure out what to do next.

It dawned on him that he had driven all this way with the most basic plan ever. Walk into the bakery, apologize, figure out how to fix things, mention the Yelp thing was being taken care of. Hope no lawyers were involved yet.

Come face-to-face with an angel?

Not on the list.

This was not the small town, cozy grandmother he'd expected to find. Where was the owner while all this was going on?

"So, is your...mom here?" he asked, figuring it was probably a family business.

"My mom?" She looked at him like he might be a little nuts. "No. No, she's not here. Why are you looking for her?"

Wow. He hadn't expected to have to track the woman down. But, this was a small town. He'd find her pretty quickly. Or maybe she could just run over here and they could meet.

"Well, yeah. I had to talk to her about some business. I just expected to find her here."

"You expected to find my mom here?"

He wasn't sure why this was such a weird idea to her. Maybe her mom didn't spend a lot of time at the actual bakery. Maybe she did all the heavy lifting, so to speak.

"Well, yeah," he said again, for lack of a better answer.

"She usually comes in after yoga." She gave him a bright smile, as if this conversation wasn't going in circles.

Spence figured cutting to the chase was his best option at this point.

"I inadvertently insulted your mom, and I want to fix it."

All the friendliness on her face shifted into a neutral position.

He kind of hated that a lot. She was so...adorable in a completely sexy way. Her little flare skirt swung around her knees as she stepped back and gave him a measuring look.

"You did?" She crossed her arms over her chest, and he wasn't sure if she knew it was a move of self-defense before she carried on. "My mom is pretty hard to insult. Pretty Zen. Live and let live kind of person. You would've had to have done something really horrible to have insulted her."

The more he thought about it, the more he realized he *had* done something pretty horrible.

After his drive and getting a look at the little shop, it was clear Starlight Harbor should be on one of his lists, and he'd figure out which one before he left. Absolutely not one with the word *tacky* in it.

He didn't do anything along the lines of charming or quaint or must-see. Most of his articles aimed for something more tongue-in-cheek or (and he was ashamed of this as he stood in front of the angel) out-and-out mockery.

But there had to be something he could write about to make up for getting it so wrong.

It was that damn singing shark all over again.

And, if he brought them some business—not just the bakery, but the whole town—it would definitely be harder to sue him.

The cute baker's assistant cleared her throat.

Right.

"I'm sure you've heard about the site that listed your town as one of the top tiny towns—"

"Tacky," she cut him off, her entire demeanor changing,

shifting to hostile. Obviously she knew what he'd done and wasn't happy about it. "It wasn't the top or the tiny or the town. It was the tacky part."

"Alliteration?" Even he heard the question mark at the end of that sentence.

"Tremendous."

"You think alliteration is tremendous?"

She gave him such a scathing look that he stepped back.

"Tremendous is a tremendous *T* word that would have described this town." She narrowed her eyes. "And my shop."

Well, crap.

"Oh. Right." Spence wasn't sure he was winning any points.

He'd walked in here expecting to find a frustrated, overrun granny—which, looking back, was just stupid. More people lived in small towns and liked cupcakes than the elderly. Instead, he'd found a tiny hurricane of torment.

How about those *T*'s?

"Well," he began, trying to get them back on track so he could head home. It had been a seven-hour drive all out in the middle of the night. And he needed to get at least part of the way home today. Sleeping in the car was definitely a budget-induced option. "I wanted to come up and try to smooth things over."

She started moving with an angry grace that was both fascinating and a bit terrifying. You typically knew if a guy was ticked off enough to take a swing, but he wasn't sure what was happening right now. Of course, he also wasn't messing with a woman who had that look on her face.

She was tiny compared to him, but at the moment he didn't doubt she could take him. Even disregarding he wouldn't hit a girl or someone that much smaller.

"Let me get this straight." She came around the counter and went right past him, pushing the chairs in and wiping down a table. She swiped the rag over it with a fierce scrub, looking like she was trying to scour the varnish off the top.

"You've come all this way, from Upstate New York to fix it?" Her words came out fast and snippy, a bit more sarcastic than Spence would have thought so much cuteness could produce.

It wasn't lost on him that she already knew where he was from. It wasn't a hard thing to figure out, but it showed she hadn't closed her computer after her comment and walked away.

Now, looking at the little old baker who was actually a beautiful and talented twenty-something with what he was fearing was a taste for revenge, he also started rethinking his previous idea of *small town lawyer*.

Crap.

"As best I can." He realized now was not the time to sound cocky or too sure of himself.

Of course, he hadn't felt any of those things since he walked into this bakery. Plus, he was still waiting to hear back from his guy at Yelp.

"As best you can?" She threw the rag down on the table and strode up to meet him toe-to-toe. Which should've looked ridiculous because she barely came to his shoulder, but instead he was pretty sure at this point she'd win whichever battle she was willing to fight.

"You're not just a minion. You're the mob boss." There was so much accusation in her voice he half expected the FBI to kick down the door, raid the bakery, and take him off in cuffs right then.

"Don't you think that's a little extreme?" Even as the words rushed out of his mouth, he realized they were the stupidest thing he could say.

"Extreme?"

She poked her finger into his chest. He looked down at

the tiny hand, wondering what he was supposed to do with that.

"Extreme?" she said again. "You sent hundreds of people after my business. My tremendous, tiny, tenacious business. I had to close my website, turn my phone off. I'm trying to deal with orders, and I'm not even sure if they're real or not. How many comments attacking me or my business on your site were there? Did you give them my company name and location?"

"No! Of course not. That's completely unethical."

How insulting was that?

She looked at him as if she was surprised he knew what the word meant.

"I *know* what ethical means."

"I'm not sure you do." She stabbed her finger into his chest again.

Spence carefully blanked his expression because there was no way the angel of vengeance would find his amusement amusing.

"You are everything that's wrong with the Internet. Pretending you're a journalist when you can't even research whether a town is tacky or not."

She walked to the door and threw it open, waving her arm across the expanse.

"Does this look tacky to you? Does anything about this look tacky to you?"

When he just stood there a wee bit, afraid to move, she stabbed a finger at the ground as if telling him to get his butt over there now.

Spence was not impressed with this move, but he figured generations of men owed it to her from all the whistling and snapping that women had put up with for centuries, so he walked said butt over and looked out onto the green.

He saw exactly what he knew he would. A cute, polished, sweet little town.

Nothing tacky about it if you took the idea of Christmas out of the equation. And even the Christmas things present were tastefully done.

Of course, he couldn't help but notice yet again that there was no one out there.

Even if these people got hate visitors, they'd be better off than before he mentioned them.

"Maybe this will bring you some business," he said hopefully, trying to defuse her anger.

"Really?" She pulled the door shut and stormed back to the edge of her café to the bus cart. As she picked up each of the cups and saucers and slammed them onto a tray, he half expected glass to start flying.

"Sure. We've had lots of places get more visitors after doing an exposé on them."

She stared at him a long moment until he was pretty sure he'd won her over. All she needed was for someone to come along and explain how this worked.

"I'll put the page back up and suggest people who are in the area stop by."

She crossed her arms, her expression starting to soften.

He had her.

"I'll mention the cake. I mean, that's a gorgeous cake." He glanced at the pastries again, wishing he'd ordered something before she found out who he was. "And then business will pick up and you won't have to worry about anything."

This was a better plan than the one he'd driven up here with—which, of course, was basically show up, apologize, get Yelp down, move on with his life, and not deal with crazy backwoods coastal locals.

"I wouldn't have to worry about anything?" she asked.

"Nope. Worries gone."

29

"You're going to save me and my little town?"

When she put it like that, she should be thanking him. Maybe he could get some affiliate agreements set up.

He gave her a reassuring smile, maybe a bit of a flirty one, too, and nodded.

"I'm sure we can do it together."

She stared at him a long moment before mumbling some letters and then pointed at her door.

"Get. Out."

7

Lyra

"AND THEN HE SAID, 'DON'T WORRY, LITTLE LADY. I'LL SAVE your tiny town and you, too."

Lyra picked up her glass of iced peach tea and downed the rest of it like it was a shot of whiskey.

"Can you imagine the nerve?" she demanded. "Does our town look like it needs saving? Do I look like *I* need saving?"

Skye and Vivian gave each other a quick glance before they smirked in Lyra's direction.

"So, he's hot?" Vivian finally asked.

Skye snorted behind her sandwich as Lyra turned a glare on Vivian.

"What's that supposed to mean?" Lyra picked her glass back up, surprised to find it empty after her whiskey-shooting it.

"Well, you always had a thing for John Wayne movies..." Vivian waved her hand to stop the rush of words. "Not John Wayne, we have heard. He is problematic."

Skye mumbled a word under her breath that was much stronger than problematic.

"But John Wayne movies, John Wayne characters... Those

you've always loved. And you just used the *pretty little lady* line." Vivian grinned, looking pretty darn proud of herself. "And thus, Mob Boss must be hot."

Lyra grimaced. She hated that when he first walked in she'd noticed.

Oh, she'd absolutely noticed. The just-right amount of swagger carrying broad shoulders around. The way he took in everything, nodding to himself as if he approved. The flop of just barely too long dark hair that nearly fell into his eyes but was halted by the black-rimmed glasses he wore like Clark Kent—who, can we stop for a minute to appreciate that Clark was hot? Lois was an idiot.

Then she noticed how he was immediately enamored with her store, his gaze glancing around at all the cute little touches she'd added to make sure this was more than just a place to get a sugar rush. It was like sitting in a friend's kitchen, relaxing and letting them spoil you.

And then he zoomed in on her cake. It wasn't often she took the time to make a nine-layer cake. She was practicing for an engagement party that she wanted to spoil the bride for.

The family had been coming to Starlight Harbor for generations, each one having at least one serviceman—and then servicewoman when Marianna had enlisted—who'd impact the holiday schedule with their deployments.

She and Marianna had hit it off when they were younger, and she was always glad when they came back.

Marianna was marrying a civilian but wanted to do it here at Starlight Harbor, a place she considered nearly as sacred as her family's local parish down in New Jersey.

So, Lyra was thrilled to see the effect her cake visually had on a guest. It gave her the confidence to try to pull this off on a bigger scale for Marianna and her husband-to-be.

After the attacks and the stress of the day before, and the

added fun of not sleeping all night, it would have been exactly what she'd needed.

And then he'd opened his mouth.

So there it was. Her story at an end. The enemy vanquished.

"And then he started stalking you." Vivian snorted.

Lyra shook her head. "Stalking me? Nope. I threw him out, and he went. I am woman."

"Okay then, Miss I Am Woman, why is he sitting out on the town square, watching your shop?" Vivian hooked her thumb toward the picture window, not bothering to slow her focus on her food.

If Lyra didn't love her and her bottomless stomach and her five-nine size six frame…

"He's out on the square?" Lyra wasn't sure what that meant beyond that he wasn't giving up and going home like she'd intended him to.

Hopefully not that he was about to launch a second attack on her.

She stood, tossing her napkin down on top of her unfinished meal.

"I'll take care of this," she said in a surprisingly low and threatening voice instead of her normal squeak, and strode toward the door.

Behind her, Skye was already scraping her chair away from the table.

"You couldn't have waited until after I finished my sandwich?" Skye asked Vivian as she watched Lyra push through the front door.

Lyra glanced both ways as she crossed the street, force of habit even though it was a one-way circle around the square. Her fingernails cut into her palms where she made tiny little fists of rage. She was going to defend her town and kick this guy to the curb.

The shock on Spence's face as he caught sight of her storming at him was nearly comical enough to slow her roll, but she was on a mission.

Save Starlight Harbor from the nasty Internet mob of *Roadside Adventures* groupies.

"I thought I told you to get out." That was strongly stated and clear. There was definitely no mistaking what she meant this time.

He raised his hands to the side, giving her the standard Confused Male look.

"I am out." He glanced around like he might be being punked or something. "Literally outside. The trees and flowers and fresh air. ... Very, very, very, very out."

"I meant out of my town. Get out of my town you... you...flat soufflé." She stomped her foot in frustrated anger.

The confused look turned to one of pure humor. He was *laughing* at her.

"You're running me out of town?"

"I thought that was clear." Lyra crossed her arms, ready for a standoff.

"Well, you can't really kick me out of a town. I haven't broken any laws. This isn't the Wild West. I'm just peacefully sitting on a park bench." He shrugged and gave her a *whatcha gonna do* look.

"I don't know how it works in New York, but we don't put up with that kind of stuff here in Maine. It's time for you to get back in your little whatever you drove in on and take off."

"Again." He shook his head. "It's a free town."

She'd had enough. She'd had more than enough. This had to be harassment. Looking to where the cars were parked on the opposite side of the street, Lyra spotted the New York plates and sprang into action.

She dodged around him, picking up his messenger bag and marching toward his car.

"Hey! What are you doing?" He caught up with her in about two steps, her much shorter legs no match for his.

"I'm putting you back on the horse you rode in on and pushing you out of town."

"Those images don't even go together." He reached down and gave his messenger bag a tug as she stepped into the street. "Give me back my belongings, or I'll call the cops."

"Oh, you just go right ahead and call the sheriff. And I'll file stalking charges. You're sitting here watching my store. That's not creepy."

"You're absolutely right, sitting outside, on a beautiful day in a park on a park bench... Facing the direction the park bench is facing... Totally suspicious behavior. You should skip the sheriff and go directly to the National Guard."

"Don't tempt me." She tugged on the messenger bag.

He wrapped the strap around his wrist, locking it to him. Stalemate.

"Give me my bag, or I'm not kidding. I'll call the police."

She was about to answer something she was positive was super pithy when a car horn beeped, the bright yellow Mustang skidding to a halt.

"Oh, geez." Lyra waited, knowing that the circus had just truly come to town and Spence was in for something now.

Whether that something would help her vanquish him or just make him keel over dead with laughter ...well, win-win really.

The new bright yellow Mustang was thrown into park and Miss Angie climbed out from behind the wheel, her little pup Captain Jack Slickpaws hopping down behind her.

"Lyra! What in the world is going on?" Miss Angie swept over in her typical garb that was half tavern wench, half hippie and glanced between the two of them. "Is this young

35

man trying to steal your bag? Because Captain Jack will take care of that." They looked down at the twelve-pound puppy running around chasing his tail where Miss Angie had tied a small Jolly Roger flag.

Yep, Lyra felt ten times safer suddenly… Not so much.

"This is *my* bag." Spence gave another tug of the strap as he glared down at Lyra.

"Yes. It is absolutely his bag. I was walking it to his car for him."

"Oh, Lyra, you've always been such a thoughtful girl. Your mother must be so proud."

Lyra smirked at Spence. She all but shouted with her eyes *This is my town, buster.* She wasn't sure he was getting the message, though, because he gave another tug on the bag. Out of the corner of her eye, she saw the sheriff and Vivian coming out of her shop.

Finally. The cavalry!

"This place is absolutely ridiculous," Spence announced as he glanced around.

His words had Lyra envisioning all the horrible articles he was picturing writing.

"This place is absolutely not horrible. And if you say it is in one of your stupid articles, I will sue you for slander."

Spence snorted. "Libel."

Miss Angie glanced between them, completely confused.

"I really don't care what it is. That's why I would hire a lawyer. To help me with the harassment lawsuit that I'm already plotting in my head."

"Oh, Lyra, is this man harassing you?" Miss Angie looked down at the pup. "Captain Jack, we might have to do something about this."

The puppy gave a sharp, joyful bark, obviously enjoying all the excitement.

Lyra glanced back to where Skye and Vivian were leaning

against the wall, laughing to themselves. What kind of serve and protect was that?

She was going to file a complaint about the deputy with the deputy.

"Lyra, everything okay here?"

Lyra glanced up to see Noah, former Army Ranger, standing with his arms crossed next to Spence. He gave her a wink. "I was just coming over to get this afternoon's dessert cookie tray."

As they stood there, a car pulled up behind Miss Angie's. They had officially reached traffic jam capacity for Starlight Harbor.

The man opened his car door and got halfway out, leaning on the doorframe. "Miss Angie, everything okay with your car?"

"Oh, Ralph, everything is great. I love my new car. I just brought her in to Vivian to make her do a little extra *vroom vroom*, if you know what I mean." The 82-year-old woman grinned as she gave Vivian a little wave.

Even Lyra was beginning to see the ridiculousness of the situation.

She glanced up at Spence, who she expected to have a mocking look of disdain on his face. Instead, he looked amused, perhaps even more at ease.

"All right, folks. That's enough. Show's over." Skye finally stepped into the road, giving a quick clap of her hands. "Don't worry, Miss Angie. I've got this."

"Skye, thank goodness you're here. This man was trying to kidnap Lyra."

"Now don't you worry, Miss Angie. No one's getting kidnapped. You just hop back into your car—which I will be sending you your ticket for driving on public roads later—and I'll take care of everything."

"I don't think you should give me a ticket, because it's

very lucky I was here to stop the event."

With a ridiculous amount of dignity for the way she was dressed and the puppy running around chasing his tail following her, Miss Angie strode back to her car, got in, and peeled out, barely missing all the pedestrians by inches.

"That woman is going to kill someone." Noah shook his head as he watched her pull away. "I hope I'm as crazy as her when I'm that age."

"Oh, honey, we all know you're that crazy now." Lyra patted him on the arm, giving it a squeeze for good measure. "No sane person jumps out of perfectly good airplanes."

The girls gave Noah, one of their town transplants, a rough time for a few minutes before someone cleared his throat.

"Excuse me. I don't mean to interrupt all the flirting and complete lack of law and order." Spence glanced between the women, seemingly more annoyed by being ignored than not. "But I'd like my bag back and to press charges for attempted robbery. And perhaps assault."

"Assault! No one assaulted you. *You're* harassing and stalking me."

"Really?" Noah all but flexed his entire upper body as he crossed his arms over his chest.

Lyra was reluctantly impressed that Spence didn't cower at the obvious attempts at guy-on-guy intimidation.

"Okay, this has been amusing." Skye's tone said she was no longer joking. "But you've ruined my lunch. We're going to take this inside. Then I'll decide if this meeting gets transferred to the police station after another cup of tea because I'm under-caffeinated and about to arrest all of you."

With that, she strode back across the street to jerk the front door of The Sweetest Things open and gave a hard, empathetic point to the group and then pointed inside.

Vivian glanced at her cell and scowled. "Well, darn it all.

I'm going to miss all the fun. I have to go pick Tyler up." She glanced at Skye and gave her a wicked smile. "I don't suppose you'd be willing to Facebook Live this to my Messenger?"

"Tempting, but no."

Vivian leaned down and kissed Lyra on the cheek. "Fight the man, Lyra. Fight the man."

Skye shook her head, obviously exasperated with everyone at this point.

Lyra tugged the bag, but Spence didn't let go. They glared at each other until Skye finally had enough.

"That's it. Give me the bag. Everybody inside."

She marched them both inside, Lyra in the lead because it was her shop and she deserved to be able to set the tone.

She'd just gained a second level of home turf advantage and was going to use it to overcome this mob boss and all he stood for.

8

Spence

SPENCE HAD BEEN WRONG. ABSOLUTELY WRONG.

This town wasn't tacky. It was crazy.

Every single one of these people was nuts.

He walked into the cool bakery, unsurprised this time by its complete charm and warmth, and headed over to where the sheriff was pulling two tables together.

He shouldn't have been surprised to see the muscle head had decided to tag along.

With his luck—and all the flirting that had been going on —that guy was dating Lyra and Spence wasn't going to make it out of there without some bones broken. Or, at the very least, broken glasses.

"Noah?" The sheriff gave him a look.

"Sorry. Cookie emergency. Can't leave until I get my cookies. You know how Mr. Cameron and Mr. Forsyth get. I don't come back with cookies and whoever loses today's game blames me... Or you."

The sheriff just groaned but gave Noah a nod. "Fine. Stay over there. Don't say anything. Not a peep, not a cough, not a growl."

It wasn't a good sign she was letting him stay. She didn't look like a woman you wanted to mess with, and she was armed. But she must be leaning toward dealing with this in a way Spence wouldn't like if she was letting backup stick around.

He took the chair closest to the door, an instinct that wouldn't do him any good with the guy guarding it. Apparently, while he'd been doing that, Lyra had put together a guest tray. She put four iced teas and a collection of sugar cookies down in front of him.

"Only one of these is poisoned," she said with a saccharine sweet smile. "You get to pick first."

Over by the door, Noah snorted.

Spence picked up the tea, looked her dead in the eye, and drank three gulps.

There was no way he was going to be threatened by a small woman handing out iced beverages and cookies. It would take a lot more than that.

Éclairs, maybe.

"Let's just figure out what's what. I'm Deputy Mackay," she introduced herself as she pulled out a notebook and set it in front of her before she took a sip of the iced tea. "Oh, nice. What happened to the peach?"

"You finished it off at lunch."

Sure, this was definitely going to be fair.

"So, Spence. Tell me about the cyber attacks on Lyra that occurred yesterday until she was forced to shut down her website, her phone, and her business."

Yep. Totally fair.

Spence thought about not taking the situation seriously because, let's be honest, this was ludicrous. But that wasn't going to get him any further, and by the looks of it, might get his butt thrown in the local pokey. Or whatever they called jail here in tiny town.

"At no time did I encourage, suggest, or direct people to attack Miss Grigor's business or person."

And, he continued in his head, she brought this upon herself by engaging. Everyone knows not to engage.

He glanced across the table at the small woman, her hands in little fists he was betting she thought carried all the power in the world.

When she'd poked him out in the park, he'd nearly laughed. That small hand trying to physically force him to do something had been so adorable. That, and the color raised in her cheeks making her freckles stand out and eyes look an even brighter green.

She was like sunshine and summer.

"And yet the harassment got so bad that I had to shut down everything last night. I may have even canceled orders that were valid, which will affect my Yelp reviews. Oh, wait." Lyra made a big impression of remembering something. "My Yelp page is now under one star... Which I didn't even think was possible."

Neither did he, come to think of it. "I'm working to take care of the Yelp situation."

Her brows went up, a bit of shock on her face. "So you admit that the situation is your fault?"

"I admit nothing."

"Yet you're here to, and I quote, fix it. And now you're taking care of the Yelp situation?"

That was enough of that. All the warm, protective feelings he'd been having just a moment ago rushed out of him. He had to remember why he was here. He basically had to save her to save himself.

"You got yourself into a situation by engaging in a community you're unfamiliar with. Because nothing like that has ever happened on my site before—" He ignored the *pfft* and kept going. "I felt, not a responsibility, but a desire to calm things down. To assist you in taking yourself out of this hole. By doing this, I also wanted to make sure that anyone else who visits my community doesn't end up in the same precarious situation."

They stared at one another over the table. He couldn't read her, but he glanced at the sheriff, who seemed a mixture of amused and committed.

"Translation: you're here because I threatened to sue you."

Spence hoped his face didn't telegraph the truth. That was absolutely why he was here.

He couldn't very well tell her he was here because he was so far in debt he couldn't see the top of the hole. That he lost sight of his dream and every day was another step further away from the life he wanted.

And he certainly couldn't tell her that one lawsuit from her could change everything he was working toward to put it all behind him and get his life back on track.

Instead, he said, "I certainly don't want to be sued. But I don't think there's anything weird about that."

They went back to their stare-off. From behind them, a deep sigh echoed. He wanted to turn around to be like *Sorry, Mr. Muscles*. Nerd boy and bakery girl can't just have a brawl and settle it that way.

The sheriff scribbled a couple notes, and he wasn't the only one trying to stretch a little to see what she was writing. When she caught them both doing it, she snapped her notebook shut and speared them both with a glare.

"I want this fixed. And I want it fixed now." She turned to Lyra and continued, "You know the town does not have time for this, especially being a Christmas weekend. Figure out what's going to make this work for you."

"Well…" Lyra drew the word out, obviously not sure what she wanted.

"Wait a second." Spence waved a hand to get the attention

back to him. "I already shut the post down and closed the comments. I'm taking care of the Yelp situation, and I came to apologize in person."

"Stalker," Lyra said under her breath.

The sheriff gave her a look and Lyra subsided, sitting back and crossing her arms. He wasn't fooled into thinking she was done fighting him though.

"You put Lyra at risk, and you insulted the town. I think you can do a little more than apologize." The sheriff gave him a look, and he realized that was not a suggestion.

"So what were you thinking?" Might as well hear the high bid right off the bat.

"You know, you mentioned exposés…"

Of course she'd remember that.

"I'm not really sure what we'd be doing an exposé on. I have done specials on small towns with long histories that were losing their ability to keep people." He shrugged. "Sometimes it helps to revitalize them, get things back on track for at least a segment of the population."

The two women looked at each other and burst out laughing. He wasn't sure what was so funny about his suggestion. He just offered them prime real estate in his magazine.

He even glanced over his shoulder at the Noah guy, who lowered his head and was swiping his fist across his jaw, apparently attempting to hide the smile.

"What's so funny?"

Both women did one of those silent conversations as only girls can do. He waited them out, knowing there was no point rushing them. When they were done, apparently Lyra had been nominated to give him whatever it was that they thought was so funny.

"Starlight Harbor isn't a dying town. Quite the contrary.

We specifically limit how many weeks a year we're available for our guests."

He was really hoping this was not one of those weeks, then.

Either way, that seemed extremely shortsighted. Wouldn't they rather use that time to make additional income?

And who were these custom guests?

"You know what? Maybe we should back up." The sheriff shook her head and glanced at Lyra in another one of those conversations. There really should be a second-language course for men. "Do you even know what we do here?"

"Sure. You're one of those places that picks a holiday and does it year-round."

Lyra rolled her eyes. "Ignoring the condescension, the simplification of the theme, and you stacking us in with places that do kitsch instead of service, you're not really that close. I mean you got the word *Christmas* in there, so eight points out of the hundred. But other than that, you're pretty far off."

"Okay." He crossed his arms and leaned back in his chair. "Explain it to me."

He all but saw her open her mouth to say she'd use small words but shut it, obviously trying to meet him in the middle.

He was big enough to appreciate that.

"From your time driving in and then hanging outside stalking me, you really don't have any better guesses?"

She sounded...disappointed. As if she expected more from him. As if he hadn't completely sunk her opinion of him just because his readers were idiots. He felt himself sitting up a little straighter and hoped muscle guy hadn't noticed.

Of course, he probably evened out that guy-move when he pushed his glasses back up his nose.

"I'm guessing you focus on little shops, maybe some whale watching." He nodded, warming up to the theme. It was cute. People did love seaside towns. "I bet there's some kick butt lobster rolls to be had. I'm assuming it isn't just the summer tourists. But, beyond that? I don't know. It looks like Christmas left dust everywhere."

He made sure to keep his voice light. No need to criticize the town for having a niche they claimed worked for them. The lights and decor had been tasteful, pretty even. Like a Hallmark movie, but way more understated.

"Yes, to all that. But that's not really the point," she continued on, starting what he knew was a history lesson he'd better listen to for the clues he needed to fix this mess and get back to New York. "We've been doing it since World War II. It started as a small thing, but—"

"He doesn't need the entire history," the sheriff stepped in, obviously trying to move things along.

Lyra scowled at her. "Of course he does, if he's going to understand what he's done."

"Right." The sarcasm was obvious.

"Fine. We can backtrack after we've let him know the entire town isn't insane."

Deputy Mackay gave a hand motion, as if to say *carry on*. "Just the pertinent facts. I think he can fill in the 'generations since World War II' stuff."

Again with the crazy.

"So." Lyra was obviously a bit thrown off having to skip decades. It was cute watching her regroup. She'd been excited to give him the whole history. "We basically have a rotating schedule of weekends where we celebrate Christmas."

Spence glanced between them, wondering if he was supposed to be able to keep up with her jump from "everything and the kitchen sink" to basically nothing.

"Okay." The sheriff sighed. "A little more than that. And when did you get so obstinate?"

"Yesterday at 10:37." After taking a long sip of tea, she turned back to Spence. "Once upon a time, many generations ago, Starlight Harbor was a town stripped of all its young men who were sent to The Great War."

"Dramatic much?" Noah asked from the doorway.

"Shush. And when Christmas came about, the town realized that nearly every family was left not only struggling because all the young men who worked the lobster boats were gone, but had absent loved ones. And so the Great Early Fathers of the town—"

"Okay, now you're just milking your ridiculousness."

"Gathered together," Lyra went on, undeterred, "and declared there would be no Christmas until the men came home to warm the hearts and homes of their loved ones."

Noah snorted. "Not sure it went down quite like that, but okay."

"And so the first Christmas went by, and the town treated it quietly as if it were any other day. But then, something they hadn't considered happened."

The sheriff all but rolled her eyes. "I'm sure mothers considered it."

Spence tried to keep up with the storyline while the barbs bounced around, but he found his attention just kept coming back to Lyra no matter what.

"They got horrible news. It had taken the Administration nearly a year to let them know of the deaths of several of their boys, because Starlight Harbor wasn't listed as an incorporated town. They'd fallen through the cracks in the worst possible way. It was only when someone was being sent home injured that the darn bureaucrats"—She shot a glare at the sheriff as she snorted again—"put two and two together and came up with… seven."

The two fell silent for a moment, and Spence considered what it would be like to find out such devastating news all in one blow. And to be part of a history so deep you still felt the sting of it generations later.

"Can you imagine?"

He shook his head. He absolutely could not. When they'd nearly lost his brother... Well, he didn't think about it, if at all avoidable. But to get hit with that much death at once...

It was unthinkable.

"The Great Town Fathers—"

"Seriously, the Selectmen."

"—gathered around the table—"

"Technically accurate."

"—and suggested that perhaps the town shouldn't wait for Christmas until everyone was home. Perhaps they should celebrate it whenever anyone came home for all the boys who missed the time to indulge in family and to remember the true spirit of the season."

Lyra glanced at the sheriff who gave her a shrug.

"And so it became a thing. Each time someone returned, the next weekend was Christmas. Sometimes that would be every other weekend. Sometimes a few months would pass. And then the surrounding towns brought their returning servicemen for the celebrations, too. When the war was over, the town suspected things would just die down, but that's not how wars work. It took forever to get everyone home. And then, of course, you had military who weren't just signed in for the big fight."

"And more wars," Noah added as he stared over their heads at something only he could see.

"Starlight Harbor decided they'd create a schedule and let those who needed a place for some Christmas recovery to come and just enjoy themselves and save that special family time for when everyone could be present. Way more personal than a five-minute Skype conversation on the holiday."

Spence glanced between them, blinking a bit. It wasn't tears. Just...he had to blink.

"Every other weekend?" he asked.

"Well," the sheriff took back over. "Not quite. We shut down as a destination for December and January. Although, we seem to be just as busy what with the weddings of people who fell in love with Starlight. And the other holidays have to be respected. Occasionally a family will request a weekend that isn't scheduled, and if they're not a small group, we can accommodate that—but we do try to make sure there's time and space on the calendar for Starlighters to go on their own vacations."

"People can't just come whenever they want?" Because, he really wasn't sure how this business plan was working for them.

"Well, sure." Lyra flashed him a wide smile. "But not every weekend is a celebration. We have carolers, the Santa Sleigh Parade, and pictures with Santa. But, we keep the holiday decorations classy so we can keep them up for guests who aren't able to make the weekends. Our wander-throughs. People from the area come in for gifts, to eat at the restaurant or cafés, grab an ice cream, and walk around. But most of the holiday stuff only comes out for the Christmas weeks."

Which explained the lights. And the signs. And the trees. And...well, everything.

"That's..." Spence shook his head.

This was worse than the singing shark.

He'd gotten this wrong in the worst possible way. This town shouldn't be mocked. Its true history couldn't be.

There was too much honor in it.

He glanced back at Lyra, her face a subtle balance of

disdain and hope. Even she hadn't given up on him getting a clue.

"I'm sorry, it sounds stupid after what you just told me." He took a long sip of the tea that may or may not be poisoned and glanced around the room. This was way more than a town. It was a mission.

"What do you think would fix this?" Because he was completely on board with making it better.

And maybe getting that smile back on Lyra's face before he had to leave.

9

Lyra

SHE FELT LIKE SHE HAD GONE TOE-TO-TOE WITH A GIANT...
And won.

Sure, this could backfire. He could end up doing an exposé that made them all look ridiculous. Because, let's be honest, the whole situation with Miss Angie and Captain Jack and their threats and Noah acting as her bodyguard had been absurd.

But continuing on with the honesty, it was also pretty accurate.

In the best possible way.

Lyra chuckled to herself as she put away her tea tray and cleaned up after their meeting. It would've been something to see Captain Jack try to take down the nearly six-foot-tall journalist.

She needed to remember to carry her phone in case she needed a photo or bribery video. Although, Miss Angie would probably be so proud of her willingness to charge into danger that there'd be no blackmail ability at all.

The soft chime of the bell over the front door rang. She

was about to shout out that she was closed for the afternoon when Skye's voice called from the front.

"Come on out of hiding! I know you're back there."

Skye stuck her head through the kitchen door and glanced at the end-of-day mess Lyra was cleaning up.

She had on her favorite 50s retro apron. It made her feel like one of her heroes...Donna Reed.

"Did you know that Donna Reed was one of the producers of her show—one of the first women producers in television??"

"Yup."

"And also that she refused for her character to only cook and clean? That she was the reason sitcoms started showing mothers being more active in the community?"

"I've heard that, too."

"And that her famous Bundt cake is the reason I became a baker?"

Skye gave a deep sigh and nodded. "True. I *have* heard all that. My bestie gets stuck on Donna Reed when she's stressed out or angry. Did you know that women who obsess over Donna Reed are more likely to blackmail journalists into positive coverage of their town online than women who don't?"

"Mock all you like, but Donna did it all in dresses and heels while forcing men to take her seriously."

"Oh, he takes you seriously, all right."

"I don't know what you're talking about." Lyra set the cooling racks aside and began doing her afternoon's ingredient inventory.

"Don't get me wrong, I think you handled him brilliantly. But I have to say, by the end I was almost feeling bad for him." Skye flashed a smile and a wink at Lyra when she gave her a hard glance. "I said *almost*. I mean, you've even got him staying with Noah. The fact Noah would volunteer to share a space with anyone, let alone a man he was willing to rip arms off of and stuff down his throat half an hour earlier, probably means he made Noah feel a little bad for him, too."

"Or," Lyra added something to her list, "Noah just wants to make sure he can keep a close eye on him. Enemies closer, etcetera, etcetera."

Skye stepped aside as Lyra breezed through, going out to check that the customer stand was stacked with napkins and everything else for the morning.

"I've been weighing the facts and can only come to one conclusion. There's an excellent chance you've gone insane."

Lyra froze, turning an angry glare on her best friend. That was above and beyond.

"Reaching my breaking point is not going insane. It's calmly stepping over the line and deciding to verbally kick his a—butt."

Skye started laughing, her eyes welling up with tears that she was brushing away before they slipped down her cheek.

"What, may I ask, is so funny?"

Skye waved her hand as she tried to catch her breath. This was not earning Lyra's patience.

Which, as stated above, was already used up completely in calmly crossing a line.

"It's just…" She sucked in a breath. "It's just, I don't think I've ever heard you say *ass* before."

Skye burst out in new laughter, obviously believing the world must be coming to an end if her "words, words, words" friend actually almost used a word that might fit on a curse list for some people.

"Why are we friends again?" Lyra pulled the drawer from the cash register and started counting out the day, which was regrettably short because of the throwdown situation.

This was costing her in more ways than one.

They needed to take some precautions to make sure Clark Kent and his beautiful brown eyes truly understood the world he'd stepped into.

And she was just the girl to do it.

Spence

"HERE YOU GO." NOAH PUSHED THE DOOR OPEN TO A ROOM AT the back of the house. "Bathroom's across the hall. I don't typically lock up on off weeks, but I'll put a key on the table for you."

Spence stepped in and glanced around at the spare but nicely finished room.

"Thanks, man. I, um…" He wasn't really sure how much to tell this guy who just opened his home to him but had been willing to beat the snot out of him an hour ago.

Of course that last part probably still held true.

Noah waved him off before he could find the words. "Seriously. Don't worry about it. It's what we do."

Before Spence could figure out how to answer that, Noah slapped him on the shoulder and headed out. "I'm going to head back to the café. I'll leave my cell number on the table. Let you get settled. Since you didn't bring anything, there's a Walmart about twenty minutes outside of town."

Spence watched him disappear out the front door and then glanced around, shocked that he was just given the run of a stranger's house.

Especially after all the things he'd been accused of in the last three hours.

Of course, finding out this guy was a former Army Ranger meant that no sane person would rip him off. But still...

Because he didn't want to live in these clothes without a shower for the next however long this was going to take, Noah's idea made sense. Spence headed back up to where he'd left his car in the square.

He wasn't above admitting that it was a great walk. The weathered craftsman cottages and the Cape Cods with their shutters that had probably seen actual use. The smell of the ocean. The subtle decorations that hinted at the celebration he'd be witnessing in a couple days. It all came together to create a charming tableau he couldn't ignore.

And, at the end of the walk was Lyra.

Okay, so technically at the end of the walk was his car. But it was parked by Lyra's shop. He was tempted to drop in, see what the bright, beautiful firecracker was up to now that she'd vanquished the mob boss.

He'd never been drawn to delicate-looking women, but the fact that she was pure steel and strength under her little dresses and hair thingies was appealing in a way he couldn't have expected.

The man on the porch who had waved to Noah as they'd walked down did the same as he passed by again.

"Here for a visit?"

Unsure what to say to that, he just nodded.

He wasn't really big on the idea of admitting that the town sweetheart had threatened to sue him. He had a feeling just the idea that she might have would be enough to have him ridden out of town in the back of a wagon, tarred and feathered old *old*-school style.

The man didn't seem offended. Just gave him a smile and went back to reading his paper.

That was something he wasn't sure he could get used to. This weird combination of being absolutely involved in one another's lives while having the same ability to completely leave one another alone when they wanted.

Was that something Mainers were born with?

He got to the top of the hill and cut across the square to his car, half of him hoping he could hop in and sneak away. The other half hoped for another round with Lyra.

Even with the arguing and the disagreements and the fact that he had wronged her so badly, he was still fascinated.

It wasn't just that she took his breath away. It was everything about her. Like how she seemed to love at full speed. Her friends, her shop, this crazy town, everything that was counted as hers was accepted and adored.

If a man were looking for something like that—

But he wasn't. Spence shook himself from the daydream.

He had to stay on mission.

Make good with the town, get his site on point to sell it, get out of debt, and start working on a career that he might be almost a decade too late to get into.

Nowhere in there was there space to woo a strawberry-haired baker.

He glanced toward her shop as he unlocked his car, wondering if he should go back in and try to leave things in a better place, less challenging than they were when he left.

No. He did the smart thing for once. Trying not to glance back as he pulled away, Spence headed toward the plaza two towns over, already trying to come up with the best way to write about a town that was crazy without making it sound crazy.

Piece of cake.

11

Lyra

LYRA WASN'T SURE THIS WAS A GOOD IDEA, BUT IT WAS THE best one she had.

If he was going to write an exposé, she wanted to make sure he saw the town the way it really was...through her eyes. As the magical place she grew up in, came to love, missed when she was away, and respected for its mission in its small corner of the world.

She wanted him to see the truth.

And then she wanted him to write about it.

That was why she had little flip-flops going on in her stomach. It had nothing to do with how stinking cute Spence was, or that he didn't look at her like she was the little sister who grew up down the street or the tiny, cute "little elf who bakes things," as she heard so frequently.

He looked at her with an intensity that sometimes made her forget her words.

She managed to get through their meeting on pure anger, but watching him soften as he learned the history of Starlight Harbor had *her* softening toward him.

Right now, though, she tightened her fists. He was the enemy.

Raising one of those fists, she knocked on the door in front of her. There was a long pause, and then heavy steps before it flew open. Noah was just there, pulling a T-shirt over himself, his hair wet.

"Sorry, end of the day. Washing the café off." He stepped aside and motioned her in. "Spence just got back from picking up supplies. I have to say, he won me over a little bit by bringing a six-pack of that new blueberry ale from Starhouse Brewery."

Lyra shook her head. Leave it to guys to be bought by a couple bottles of alcohol.

"We're out on the deck." Noah gave her a head nod, guy speak to follow him through his craftsman to the back of the house. A slider led out to a deck, still high enough on the hill up from the water to give a great view of the harbor.

"This is great. Why have I never been here before?" She looked up at him with accusing eyes, then batted her lashes for good measure.

Noah shook his head. "I just finished the deck in May. Only Jamie and Cam have been out here."

Right. That would've made all the difference. Lyra rolled her eyes. Noah was considered the eligible bachelor of the moment.

He was one of the few business owners in town not from Starlight Harbor and there seemed to be this small wall built around him, even as he spent all his time caring for the town and its occupants. Almost as if he didn't expect the care to go both ways.

Note to self: she'd have to be a better friend. And not like the women who made it their mission to get the attention of the ranger who seemed to dodge all of the grabby hands and numbers on napkins. And not just from the locals.

Then she turned, and her gaze caught Spence's.

He sat there, jet-black hair falling forward, sweeping across the top of his black-framed glasses, that dark gaze she kept feeling on her whenever they were together—

both curiosity and challenge.

And then he smiled.

Her stomach did another flip-flop.

"Lyra. Is something else wrong?" He pushed away from the table and came around to meet her. "More trouble? Is it your website? Because I can take care of that."

Oh, no.

That was unexpected. It felt like…like he actually cared and not just that he didn't want to get sued.

"I just thought—well, Vivian suggested, and it made sense that I come by and see if you need anything or if you wanted to do a tour of the town. Walk around a bit and get the highlights before the guests show up tomorrow."

He stared down at her, so close she was surprised he'd gotten within her personal space without her noticing until she stopped talking.

And then, the right side of his mouth kicked up, a grin that wasn't mocking or defensive. Just one that seemed to say —*things*.

"That sounds great. I drove around when I first got here, but a tour is exactly what I need. Plus, I don't want to be in your way while people are here." His hand came up, and just for a moment she thought he was going to touch her. Instead, he ran it through his hair and glanced down at the water. "Let me grab my camera. I have some shots I'll get before I leave, but I don't want to miss anything that might just happen."

He grinned like a kid given a toy and hurried into the house.

"He's not horrible." Noah stood looking down at her with a knowing smile on his face. "I think just a little lost."

Lyra could feel the sides of her mouth kicking up at that. It was what people had said about Noah when he'd moved to town.

"Stop it," he warned. "You're doing that chick thing where everything works out happily in the end for the dude when she comes along and arranges his world for him."

Lyra went up on her toes and patted him on the cheek. "Don't worry. We'll find someone to arrange your world, too."

Before he could respond, Spence came back out on the deck, a frown line between his eyes as he glanced between them.

"Ready to go?"

Lyra's gaze bounced from him to Noah, the other man trying to hide the smirk on his face as they gave each other a long look.

Guys. Who even knew what they were thinking? They claim to be all straightforward, speak their minds and stuff. But that look was way over her head...figuratively and literally.

Instead of making a snarky remark, she swept by Spence and toward the front of the house.

He opened the front door for her and nearly pushed her out as Noah shouted from the deck, "Curfew's at ten."

She wasn't positive, but she was pretty sure that Spence gave Noah a gesture he wouldn't have if she were facing them.

And, like womankind before her, she ignored their idiocy and moved on.

"Settled in? You've got what you need for a couple days?"

"Yup." He gave a nod, glancing around as if orienting himself before moving on.

"Great. So…" This had seemed like a good idea at the time, but now she wasn't sure where to start.

They paused at Water Street, the road that ran straight down from the Town Hall on the square to the water, each side branched with occasional little shops backed by centuries-old cottages.

Boy, she'd already blown the plan. She wasn't sure where to take him at all. There was just so much to see.

"Why don't you bring me to your favorite spot besides your bakery and tell me about it?"

Relief flashed through her. Of course he'd know how to start. This is what he did.

"Right. This way." She turned to head down to the harbor. "I grew up here. We traveled a little, but my dad left when I was four. I'm the youngest of three, so the town is really most of what I know about the world. That sounds dumb. I'm not an idiot. I went to college in Rhode Island and studied in Paris for a year before coming back. But we didn't do vacations all over the place. A week in Arcadia. Driving down to my mom's family in Rhode Island. So most of my favorite places in the world are here."

"Paris, huh? I loved Paris. I got to spend a week there on my way to Asia the year before senior year. It was more of a rush of night clubs, museums, and hostels than a tour of the great cafés, though."

"Oh, I don't want to say you missed out, but you totally missed out. I'm still trying to perfect my croissant."

"That's not what I heard." He grinned and she glanced up at him, wondering exactly what he'd heard that was so great. "On your Yelp page, they—"

He cut himself off, his gaze dashing from hers out to the water below them. A rush of red painted his neck from the collar of his T-shirt up.

Lyra watched him realize what he'd just said and its

implications. She knew in her heart of hearts that even if his site were responsible for what had happened to her business, he actually would never have personally created the situation himself.

She would place money on the fact that if he'd known what would happen with this article, he would have done it differently.

It was clear from what he'd said as they discussed details for the exposé earlier that he was not just put out that he was having to do this, but deeply, deeply embarrassed. Perhaps even ashamed.

Of course, she was also sure that he put some of the weight on her as well. And true, maybe she should know better how to live on the Internet.

People needed to get off the Internet.

He was here, looking to help, even if he was trying to split the responsibility in a different way than she would, so she was willing to move forward.

And, no. That wasn't the flip-flops speaking.

"Why don't we put that aside for the next couple days and handle it like you would any of your travel things."

He grinned, more sheepishly than he had before. She was surprised. It was a look she hadn't see on him. Defensive, angry, frustrated… The only one she'd seen that was positive was the way he'd looked at her cake.

And, for that moment, before it all went sideways, the way she thought he was looking at her.

"Tell me about your time in Paris."

She paused, surprised by the detour. But, maybe knowing where else she'd been would help him to see her home more clearly.

"It was just the year. I went to Johnson & Wales, so I came home fairly regularly." She'd known after one semester that she was there to study and stretch but that Starlight Harbor was her home. "My mother expected me to stay for good when I left for my semester in Paris. My brother's job keeps him on the road and at events most of the year, and my sister is an import-export specialist."

She internally rolled her eyes at that. She still bet spook.

"That's still a lot more traveling than some people." He followed her as she turned and led him down the sidewalk alongside the docks.

"Paris is beautiful, but it doesn't have the ocean." She waved a hand in front of them at the view. "I never understood how people could live without this. Not just how beautiful it is, but everything. It's constant and changeable at the same time. It brings the town its income and threatens it with storms. The harbor has us snuggled in safely, so we forget we're completely exposed. And just beyond that horizon? Is forever."

She glanced up at him and saw his gaze track up toward the horizon. He stared out over it with a new sort of wonder that surprised her. She felt herself warm. The idea of someone standing here on Starlight Point looking out and really seeing the ocean for the first time was humbling.

Gazing out, she wished she could see it anew without losing how her entire being was tied to it.

"Maybe you should be the writer. The exposé is all there in your head already."

Laughing, she swatted at him, knowing the joke for what it must be. She knew where her gifts lay: sugar, flour, and eggs were her keyboard and words.

It was easy to talk about something when you loved it to someone who is willing to listen.

She shouldn't have been surprised when Spence took the camera wrapped sideways across his chest up to his gaze and clicked away furiously.

"It never works the way I want, but I hope that I can get a

little bit of your forever in that picture." He turned his attention back on her, still sharp and focused and potent, the cocky look of a man doing what he was good at and loved.

"Where is it you're taking me?" Spence asked as he eased the camera back down to his side.

Lyra smiled and tried not to blush, because the place they were going she'd never taken anyone before.

Part of her hoped he wouldn't put it in his story, even going so far as to consider asking him not to. But she knew to truly show him Starlight Harbor, she had to show him the magic. And to do that, she had to bring him to one of the places that held her heart, kept it safe when she was away, and welcomed her home with open arms.

She reached out and took his hand, letting those feelings flow out of her.

Here she was, asking him to become a believer, and the first step in that was having someone believe in him.

Lyra asked her heart if she could be that person. Could she believe in him?

She was afraid the answer was more of a yes than she was willing to consider yet.

12

Spence

SPENCE NEARLY JUMPED OUT OF HIS SKIN WHEN HE FELT HER small hand wrap around his larger one, surprised to feel how strong they were with the little calluses on the tips from where she worked her baker stuff all day.

And then, something absolutely crazy happened. A feeling of safety and well-being like he hadn't experienced since he was young swept over him.

He had been expecting to find nothing in Starlight Harbor except frustration and anxiety. And yet here he was, getting sidetracked by exactly the person he couldn't let distract him.

But, with an instinct he was sure he could rely on, he knew Lyra wasn't using her adorable sexiness to get him to do things the way she wanted.

He gave himself permission to shake off his doubt, allow himself to accept that today—even if it was just for today— he could trust that this feeling of happiness he felt with her was something of a gift for him to enjoy.

A connection that few people got to experience with such fresh newness.

His parents had been like that. Even his dad laughingly admitted that he spent two minutes in his mother's presence and just "gave up the fight."

He'd always thought they were joking, but here he was, literally giving up a fight for her. Sure, he could still get his site sold and himself out of debt if he could just make the stars align with this exposé.

He'd been so focused on the future, all of it shrouded in negativity, that this time with her was like an emotional vacation. He promised himself that no matter what, he would do justice to the little town she loved so much.

"Tell me about this magic place you're going to show me." He slid his hand round to settle it more firmly in hers.

Maybe she hadn't meant to take his hand. Maybe it was just to get his attention. But he realized, once it was there, he had no plans of letting it go.

Today. He reminded himself. He had no intention of letting it go today.

"To the lighthouse."

She pointed out to the edge of the harbor to a lighthouse, its red stripes setting off against the sky in a quintessential New England pattern.

"Can we get to it from here?" he asked.

"Only if you're up for it." She gave him a saucy grin. "It's a hike, and the only other way out is through Mr. Ross's yard. Which is an absolute no-go. Even now that we're not kids."

"Does he live in it?"

She shook her head and turned them down the road that ran parallel with the shore, waving to the men working on the docks as they brought in their afternoon catches.

"No. Not in years. There's a house on the property. The road goes to the house, and there's a path he can take an ATV or sled out to it in any weather."

"It does take a bit away from the romance of it all."

"Have you ever been inside a lighthouse? There's not a lot of romance to most of them. Especially here in Maine where so many of them are on a crag instead of on the mainland. At least here the keeper had rooms inside before the town built the house."

"So, no romanticizing the lighthouse."

She gave him a shy smile. "We'll see."

The docks fell away, and a few smaller cottages with big decks faced the water.

"I bet those are great at sunrise." He pointed at the two cottages.

"The mini-inns?" She glanced back at them as the paved road turned to dirt. "They're town rentals."

"The town owns rentals?"

"Yup. For overflow for large families who fill the inn to capacity or small families who want privacy." She gave him a sad smile. "Often people coming home don't want to be in an open setting, and if we can't promise the innkeeper is the only other person there, they'd rather have the smaller spaces and make their own meals."

Spence *mm-hmm*'d, because what were you going to say to that?

"We also have families who return off schedule to relax somewhere familiar. And, we've had our share of memorial services since this might be the last time a service person got to spend time with their family before they lost them."

At the catch in her voice, he gave her hand a small squeeze.

He was such an idiot, simplifying something far more important and beautiful than he knew.

He cut himself some slack because there was no way he could have known, but still. It was his job to verify things before he shot off his mouth.

Or in this case, his website.

The dirt road turned to a sandy path then to dunes. Lyra leaned over and pulled her little girly dress sneakers off and waited while he followed suit. He couldn't remember the last time he'd walked anywhere barefoot outside his own apartment. There was something amazing about feeling the sun-heated sand shifting under his feet, sliding between his toes.

He realized she was watching him make mouse-size sand dunes with his feet when Lyra laughed at him. Spence was surprised to feel another rush of heat on his neck. He wouldn't have thought he was young enough to blush anymore, but here he was, feeling the pink on his cheeks as sure as if he were seventeen.

It was this girl, this crazy amazing girl.

Before he could do anything, say anything even, she turned back and was running up the dune, sand flying in her wake. He took a moment of enjoyment to watch her long, bare legs fly, her skirt flip back and forth over them, as she reached the top and laughed back down at him.

She was already turning to drop over the other side as he rushed after her, the sand shifting beneath his feet in more ways than one.

At the top, he saw the long stretch of rocks with a sharp drop to the water and an open plain of sea grass out to the point where the lighthouse stood, a beacon for a blue-on-blue horizon.

Up ahead, Lyra stood, the wind whipping her hair and skirt behind her as she looked back, her hand blocking the sun from her gaze and wavering him on.

Instead of rushing to catch up, he raised his camera and shot. Just one picture before she laughed and turned to keep going.

He didn't need to look to know it was perfect.

He was a little afraid that she was right. From up here, you could see forever.

Lyra

LYRA TURNED AND WALKED THEM ALONG THE EDGE OF THE cliff where the sand met the rock, pointing out to Spence the places he should be careful of loose gravel or sand making it easy to slip.

"You used to come out here alone when you were young?" he asked, a bit in awe. "You were a little daredevil."

Something about the ridiculous version of her pasted a happy grin on her face. She'd always been the good child, the easy child. The sweet little girl.

Her brother grew up to be a rock star and her sister grew up to be in the CIA.

Or that import-export business Lyra was sure she used as a cover.

The daredevil tag would never be put on her compared to the other two. It was nice to look a little dangerous in someone's eyes.

"It was a secret. So no one knew I was a daredevil."

They came around the backside of the lighthouse, and she turned him toward the ocean.

"That view, right? You should see it when a storm is

coming in. A Nor'easter. It's like a wall of destruction coming at you, and you're out here and for a moment you forget that there's a whole world behind you. Instead it's just you and the lighthouse and the storm."

She leaned against the sun-heated outer wall and glanced up to where Spence copied her actions.

"Did you do that a lot?" he asked. "Sneak out to watch a storm come in?"

"Not as much as I would have liked. My brother and sister used to accuse me of wandering off too often, so they'd be aware of my absence."

"What about your parents?"

"When my dad left, it was just us and my mom. And my mom is kind of…she's a free spirit."

"How can you be a free spirit with three little kids?"

"Well, that's the thing about free spirits. They don't typically realize they have responsibilities. They think those things are optional. We're lucky she was responsible enough and we lived in probably the safest town in the world."

"Except for those Nor'easters," he answered with a grin.

"Except for."

He patted the wide base and leaned his head back, looking up, up to the widow's walk circling the lantern room.

"Did you ever go in?"

Lyra smiled, not because she had gone in—which she definitely had—but because no one else would have asked that. The lighthouse was strictly off-limits, and for some reason it was one of the rules all kids followed. All but her apparently.

Looking back, it was surprising she hadn't run into anyone here looking for a space for privacy as teenagers. Late at night, after the games…

Not that anyone would have ever thought to bring Lyra

Grigor out for that kind of privacy. Nope. She was every-one's little sister.

"Yup." She peeked up at him from under her lashes. "Mr. Ross moved out about fifteen years ago."

She closed her eyes, pushing at the idea that after fifteen years she finally brought someone here. Not for romance. Absolutely not. Because she needed him to understand Starlight Harbor like she did, to completely fall in love with it. But she wasn't sure she was being honest with herself.

"This lighthouse has quite the history." She glanced up to make sure she had his attention. "You've heard about Starlight Harbor's most current tradition. But there's an older tradition that goes back centuries, not just generations."

"All right, Cupcake. I'm not gonna lie. It sounds very intriguing. But can you live up to the hype?" Spence grinned down at her, obviously teasing.

"I'm pretty sure I can. And this lighthouse plays a huge part in that history." She slid down the wall until her butt hit the ground and tucked her skirt around her knees, waiting for Spence to join her on the foundation. "Starlight Harbor was founded centuries ago by several families from a few clans in Scotland who were struggling against extinction during the British clearances. Together, they came and founded Starlight Harbor, which back then had a nearly unpronounceable Scottish name."

"My Gaelic isn't too bad. Want to give it a try?" Spence asked.

"Really?"

"Nope, not even close. Totally joking. I don't think I even know yes or no."

"It's not just *aye* and *nae?* Have I learned nothing from *Outlander?*"

Spence laughed at her and made a motion to continue.

"One of the things that these couple of close clans were known for was their ability to thrive on a rocky coast, to catch a boat full of fish even in the roughest seas, and to be able to ride those seas at night around the taxman running everything from wool to whiskey to French brandy to wine."

"Let me guess. A fresh start on a completely new continent was no reason to stop with the tradition that went back too far to count?"

"However did you know?" Lyra was enjoying her opportunity to play tour guide more than she expected. She still wasn't willing to admit how much that was because of her audience.

"Lucky guess." Spence laughed, knowing that neither one of them believed that. "How does the lighthouse play into it?"

"A lighthouse's job is obvious: act as a warning system for boats about rocky or dangerous coastlines. A very pragmatic building, this lighthouse." She reached up and patted the side of the building with affection.

She couldn't help but notice that his grin seemed interested, maybe in more than her story? Not as if he was humoring her like so many of the people in her life did when she spouted her more romantic ideas.

Of course, her sister said she got that from their mother.

"I take it this lighthouse is more than just pragmatic."

"My forefathers probably thought it was when they sent off wool and received whiskey," she pointed out. "It's easy in Starlight Harbor to romanticize smugglers. They weren't pirates and felt no one was getting hurt but the taxman, who they swear was out to harm them anyway. They were nearly destroyed by a country that claimed taxes were one of the few things they wanted but instead tried to bring them near extinction. You can see why they might think smuggling was a continuation of the good fight."

With a sweep of the hand, she brought his attention back

to the sky, the water, the shape of the coast. Spence had been staring out at the ocean, and she could only guess what he was thinking.

The mysteries of the sea, the battle to keep things for your people, the harsh landing shores that would have been here before the town softened up the Inner Harbor. All those things went along with the adventure and danger of smuggling.

Like she said, it was easy to romanticize.

She thought she was ready for any of the questions he might have, to be able to answer them in a way that would appeal to the journalist in him.

Until Spence finally dragged his attention back to her and asked, "Is that why that lady was dressed like a tavern wench?"

Okay. Maybe not that one.

14

Spence

THIS WAS TURNING OUT TO BE MORE THAN A TOUR.

Today may not have started out perfect, what with the driving since the middle of the night to get here, being attacked by a small contingency of Lyra-supporters, having to go through whatever that was in the bakery and was now living with some ex-military guy who went from threatening his life in very subtle, nonverbal ways to letting him crash at his place.

But the second half, this part right now?

Now he was sitting on one of the most picturesque coasts he'd seen not just in this country, but in the world, with one of the most beautiful women. Maybe being threatened with a lawsuit wasn't the worst thing that ever happened to him.

"So." Lyra nudged his shoulder before she stood and offered him a hand. "Want to go in?"

"For real?" He'd been in ancient temples and sacred grounds, old prisons and lost graveyards, and yet for some reason the idea of sneaking into the lighthouse with Lyra sounded like one of the most exciting things he'd done in forever.

The idea of doing something off-limits with her had added a certain level of excitement to it.

"I saw Mr. Ross heading to the pub when I was walking to Noah's. Even if he just went to get a burger, he still has to go out and around to get back to his house. Get a move on."

Spence took her hand, feeling the small tug as if she could lift him off the ground by the power of her mighty little hands and willpower alone. Once up, he wrapped his hand around hers more tightly. He wasn't giving up that little treasure just because he'd gotten to his feet.

Together, they made their way to the side of the lighthouse, and Lyra let go to move a rock off where a small, lined box hid a key.

"Wait here." She ran around and unlocked the door, then returned to stash the key back in its spot.

Spence wanted to take her hand again, but she turned and flounced off to the front of the lighthouse before he could make the move.

"The lighthouse was built in 1792. It's had its share of repairs and one out-and-out rebuild, but it's remarkable what the shape and strong building material and workmanship can do. It took four years to build, and we didn't even have any federal money then. Portland got all that." As they stepped in, she propped the door open with a piece of driftwood, letting the sunshine stream past and light their way. "This first level is the original. It's been used for storage and as the jail."

"The jail? Really?" Spence glanced around thinking about what it would be like to be locked in here.

"Right? The keeper's quarters are the level below the lantern room. The original town used to spread out behind the lighthouse and up toward the road you probably wound around on if you took the highway in."

"Did you guys lock up anyone famous?" Because his readers would love this stuff.

"Local famous, absolutely. There was a pirate who kept running blockades on the smugglers, stealing their stuff, then selling it at a ridiculous price on the black market."

"Sweet."

She grinned up at him, catching the fever of her own tale. "They ran her aground and tossed her in here with a small amount of supplies for a week before allowing a trial. Basically, the lantern room ran out of wood and the lighthouse keeper was running out of food, so they finally let her out."

"Her, huh?"

"We have a long history of butt-kicking women."

"So I've learned."

"And then, when they thought—"

A tiny shadow came across the doorway and Lyra spun around.

"No!" Lyra rushed to the door as the little dog looked up at them, one eye hidden by a pirate's eye patch, and then gave the driftwood a nudge. "Captain Jack, don't you even—"

With another tiny shove of the paws, the driftwood collapsed and the heavy door pushed it into the room, cutting off all the light with a loud, echoing *boom!*

The echo died out and Spence listened for Lyra on the other side of the darkness.

"Lyra?" Spence was pretty sure he had the room mapped in his head. Most of the supplies were stacked against the wall to his left where the spiral staircase was that climbed the outer wall.

Lyra, if she made it to the door, was roughly six feet in front of him.

"I'm over here," she called.

"At the door?"

"Hold on." Feet shuffling on cement sounded and he

knew she was scooting herself the rest of the way to the door. "Yup, found it."

He followed her voice.

"Great! See, nothing to worry about. Do you need a hand?"

He reached out for her, finding her shoulder first, a small slip of hair sliding through his fingers as he did. She gave a shudder and what sounded like it might be the swallowing of a little sob.

And then, because it was the most natural thing in the world, he pulled her into his arms and ran his hand down her back.

"It's okay. You found the door." He gave her a squeeze. "My hero."

Her head hit his chest and she laughed out a frustrated sound.

"Not so much." Lyra sighed again, and he tightened his grip, wanting her to know that she was safe. "Remember how this used to be a jail? That means you need the key to get out, too."

It took Spence a minute to realize what she was saying. He didn't know whether to laugh or cry.

"You mean the key that we just rehid outside?"

"Yup. Outside. With Captain Jack, the most trouble-making dog in the world."

Spence's brain kicked into overdrive. He'd been in far worse situations than being trapped in a lighthouse with a beautiful woman.

"We're okay and we're safe, so there's no reason to panic."

"I'm not panicked." Her voice went up on the end and he tried to figure out exactly how panicked she was.

"We'll just call the sheriff—" He stopped and changed gears when she squeaked. "Noah, then. He seems like a guy who will give us a rough time but keep this to himself if *you* asked."

Which definitely brought him back to what would Noah *not* do for her.

"Probably," she allowed.

"So, you guys..." He assumed they weren't dating now, because he knew a woman like Lyra wouldn't be so friendly with him if they were. But maybe kind of dancing around dating. Or maybe dated in the past and one of them regretted the breakup?

Maybe her?

"What?"

"We should call Noah. He'll come let us out before anyone even knows we were in here." No need to get into that stuff now while they were locked together. She nodded against him again before slipping out of his arms. "You have your phone on you, right?"

"Yes. And Noah on speed dial, so easy peasy."

Spence tried not to growl at the idea of her and Noah, but it was looking more and more likely.

That's probably why Noah offered him a room, so he could keep an eye on the person his hopefully-girlfriend was threatening to sue. And who could blame him? It was exactly what Spence would do. If he had someone like Lyra to care for, he'd make sure no one messed with her, too.

Not that he was messing with her, he reminded himself. That had been a perfect storm of situational junk.

And he was absolutely going to straighten it out.

After a moment, the pale glow of Lyra's phone lit up her face. As soon as it did, a bright smile burst through like a flash of sunrise before it dropped.

"No service." She held the phone right up to his face so he had to back away to see it. "Zero bars. How can there be zero bars?"

"Is it because we're out on the point or trapped in the lighthouse?"

"I'm hoping it's because we're in the lighthouse. But honestly, I don't use my phone when I'm out here. This is my place to not use my phone." She flashed the light around, making a quick, glancing check of the base room. "Since the lighthouse is locked, maybe we can get to the top? Maybe the rooms above aren't locked?"

"You never went up?" Spence was completely surprised by that. The little daredevil wouldn't check out the highest part of the lighthouse? He couldn't imagine her just opening the door coming inside and saying, *Okay! That's enough.*

"When I was younger I did. Before it was locked because we had fewer tourists then and people worried less. I haven't been up in years, because, well…" A pale blush painted her freckled nose as she glanced away. "This is, or at least used to be, someone's house. Once I started thinking about that, it felt kind of… "

She shrugged.

This girl was adorable.

But, adorable wasn't going to get them out of the lighthouse without the entire town knowing.

"We don't really have an option now. It's not like we're snooping. We just need to get out." In the dim light, Spence could just barely make out a shadow where the circular staircase started up on the other side of the wall. "Why don't we head up? We'll skip the innkeeper's rooms as much as possible, go right to the top, and call Noah. I'm sure he'll be here as quickly as he can."

Spence tried to keep the bitterness out of his voice on that last part. Because of course he would.

She gave a nod and set her hand against the wall to follow it around the edge. "Found them."

They started up the stairs together, his hand on her lower back as she kept the cell phone screen off to save the battery.

They climbed past a couple small floors and then a latched door that cut into the steep, narrow staircase.

"So how do they make the light come on and off now? Like, why doesn't anyone live here?"

Lyra laughed. "Well, I was going to leave that out of the story because all of the romanticizing. But, computers."

Spence laughed at the ridiculousness of it. Of course, computers. It wasn't like the lighthouse was out in the water or miles away from anything and couldn't be reached if something happened. The keeper's cottage was probably sixty feet from it, and he could check whatever he needed without even leaving his living room.

Lyra climbed up and out of the stairwell at the top, the mesmerizing swish-swish of her skirt keeping his gaze following her.

He was about to tell her to give Noah a call, when he broke the top of the staircase to the lantern room.

"Wow." Spence's heart nearly dropped at the view. It went on forever, just like Lyra said. The water got darker and darker as it blended with the sky on a point so remote he couldn't guess how far away it was.

"Right?" Lyra turned around and pointed west. "Totally different view, but just as amazing."

He heard people describe the Maine coast as majestic, and now he'd never be able to deny it. This was a view that caught in his brain and tugged at his heart as well.

Lyra's voice grabbed his attention. "Hey, Noah. How are you?" She sounded way too perky. Any sane man would know she was up to something. "No, no of course I'm okay." Yup. "We just ran into a small snag in our tour. What? No, he's been perfectly nice."

She blushed and glanced up at Spence to give him a smile. He avoided rolling his eyes, but it was a darn near thing.

"Well, see the thing is," she continued, "we kind of got ourselves locked in the lighthouse... Right? Who knew you could get in the lighthouse? Shocker."

She was the worst liar on the face of the planet.

"Great, yeah, so if you could just come up to the point, there's a key... Ha ha ha." She forced a laugh at who knows what Noah said. "Anyway, the key is on the north side under a rock in a box. You kind of can't miss it because we moved it around. So, we'll see you when you get here. Drive safe!" She hung up before he could respond.

"So, Noah?"

"On his way. We should be out of here in, like, twenty minutes."

She gave one more sweep of the horizon, a small smile on her face as she turned and headed downstairs. Ignoring the torn feeling he had to stay there, drinking in the horizon, he hurried after her with the quick thought that he'd follow her anywhere.

15

Lyra

IF A GIRL COULD DIE OF EMBARRASSMENT, LYRA WAS PRETTY
sure she was walking that line right now.

Lyra wasn't sure when the last time she felt this
stupid was.

She couldn't even figure out why she thought it was a
good idea to bring him here, let alone bust into the lighthouse and... Do what?

She knew part of it had to do with proving to him that
Starlight Harbor was a town worth honoring, not mocking.
But seeing how quickly he'd accepted the town's history and
traditions had gone a long way in making her like him.

Also, the whole Clark Kent thing.

The Brandon Routh Clark Kent with the floppy hair and
searing dark eyes.

She didn't know what would happen if this exposé didn't
work to repair the damage he'd done. Noah had had a good
point that just telling his people to stop wouldn't make it
happen. She knew Noah was right and there would need to
be more to it than *Hey, guys, don't be mean to the baker girl.*

Between the two of them they would have to make an

article that walked the balance between getting the harassment to stop and not creating havoc for the rest of the town.

If they had an influx of gawkers ruining the peace they offered their guests, they'd never forgive her.

She started down the stairs, listening to him close the door behind him and checking the latch. She liked the thought of that too, not just the closing but the checking.

She always had a thing for considerate people. Probably because she hadn't grown up with any in her house.

She shook her head. What kind of idiot is attracted to consideration? Especially from someone who was here because he'd shown none.

She had to get her head back in the game.

They passed the next landing with the windows, the innkeeper's rooms. As they started past the next floor, the bright lights turned to shadows and then darkness.

"Does your cell have enough battery to light the rest of the way?"

She'd wanted to save the battery, but Noah wouldn't let them down. That guy was so solid, he was granite.

Since making sure they didn't fall down the stairs and die seemed more important than making a phone call, she flipped the screen back to on. At the bottom of the stairs, she and Spence made their way back to the door. It'd only been a few minutes, but they might as well be ready to bolt when Noah got there.

Spence had a broad smile on his face, like a little kid in a candy shop.

Or a cupcake shop if you were her.

"This place is amazing." He ran his hand along the wall and then gave it a quick *knock knock*. "I can't believe I've never been in a lighthouse. How is that possible?"

Here they were trapped in a former jail, and he was having the time of his life.

Lyra, not so much.

"I just wanted you to see how great Starlight Harbor is." She could hear the frustration in her voice. "I wanted you to see it through my eyes."

"And so you brought me to your favorite secret place." Spence gave her a smile she could just barely make out in the cell phone light. "You're willing to risk sharing your favorite place to get your town's reputation back."

"It wasn't all that altruistic. I wanted to stop the attacks on my business. That's not exactly selfless."

"You could've done that with the review of your store. But you wanted more than that. You wanted to defend the honor of Starlight Harbor against the evil overlord of the Internet. Also known as the mob boss." He laughed, even though the joke was clearly on him.

"I am sorry about that." She looked down at her feet. "I don't know what came over me. I'm usually the mellow one."

Spence laughed at that. "The mellow one? Oh no, you don't, Miss Starlight Cupcake. There's nothing about you that's mellow. That's far, far too bland a word for you. You're brave and sassy and strong. You're the daredevil."

"You've gotten the completely wrong idea about me. My best friends are brave, strong women who run their own businesses and don't take anything from anyone. My family? You haven't met my mother yet—"

"Yet?" The right side of Spence's mouth kicked up in a little grin and Lyra realized what she just said.

"Not that you have to meet my mother." Nervous chatter rushed out of her. "I'm not saying, you know, come home and meet my mom. Like the family. Not that this is a date. This is not a date. It's a tour. And I'm just, you know, showing you the town."

Spence took a step closer, his hand coming up to cup her cheek. "Why couldn't it be a tour *and* a date?"

"Oh, because..." Lyra glanced away, completely unsure what to do with that.

Was he asking or suggesting or saying or just letting her off the hook because she had become a rambling mess?

Sugar.

Sugar, sugar, sugar, sugar.

He leaned in, his gaze never leaving hers.

Her heart was going to jump out of her chest and ping around the inside of the base room like a mushy pinball leaving little flying doves and hearts in its wake if he kissed her.

"Because..."

There had to be a reason. He was her arch enemy yesterday.

"It's just that..."

"Hmmm?" he asked, smiling down at her.

"Oh, um, Noah?" She wasn't sure if the fact Noah was on his way was a real reason or a panic button.

He froze. Inches from letting his lips graze hers.

"Noah?" It sounded like a question, but she couldn't be sure.

"He—"

The door behind her flew open with a heavy thud and the man himself stood there looking back and forth at them, a suspicious look on his face.

"I'm not interrupting anything, am I?"

Sugar.

"Of course not. Thank goodness you're here. And...so quickly. What did you do, drive over the dunes?"

Noah ushered them out and sent Spence around to put the key back.

"I was heading back into town from some errands, so I was nearby." Noah gave her a grin. "Lucky, right?"

"Yup. Lucky."

The ride to her place was quieter than expected. Lyra couldn't get the almost kiss out of her head and wondered if she was nuts for not grabbing him and kissing him or avoiding it because they were in a…something.

Business agreement? Scuttlebutt? War?

Okay, maybe not the last one.

Noah finally pulled up to her door and threw the truck in park.

"Thanks, Noah." She leaned over and kissed him on the cheek before turning to hop out only to find Spence there, holding her door with a frown line between his eyes. "I'm so sorry I got you trapped in a centuries-old jail."

She wasn't sure what to do with that frown, but the longer he stared at her, the more it worried her.

"Best prison sentence ever." He looked like he wanted to say more, to do more. But then he glanced at Noah and scowled. "I'll see you tomorrow."

He hopped in the truck and gave a wave as she backed away to her door.

As the dust settled from behind them, Lyra crossed her arms and watched the headlights disappear around the corner and realized she'd been left here alone with no idea what was going on.

Now she was the one scowling.

16

Spence

NOAH THREW THE LAND CRUISER INTO PARK, TURNED OFF THE ignition, and glanced over at Spence.

"Go ahead," Spence said, knowing Noah had plenty of things he wanted to say and still wondering what was going on between him and Lyra.

He didn't want to put anyone in that situation no matter how interested he was.

Spence stopped himself right there. He lived an entire day's drive away. Last time he made the drive was the middle of the night, and even then it had been way too long with way too many trucks cutting him off for no reason.

So, he needed to let it go. Right?

Either way, he knew that there were things that were going to be spelled out for him. It might not hurt to listen and let himself hear it all from someone else as well.

"Might as well get it over with."

"You're not getting off that easy." Noah hopped out of the older model Land Cruiser and headed toward the house, glancing over his shoulder to make sure Spence wasn't far behind. Inside, he tossed the keys on the counter and kept going shouting toward the rear of the house, "We're back."

Well, that was ominous.

Spence had a feeling he wasn't allowed to just divert himself into his borrowed room or head out for a walk.

He didn't even know who the people on the other end of Noah's announcement were.

They stepped onto the deck where two guys stood around a grill. One flipped a steak and checked some potatoes in foil as the other leaned against the rail, giving him the once-over.

Three to one. There were worse odds.

Of course Noah wasn't just former army, but a former Ranger... And who knew what superpowers these other two had.

How far was it over the rail of the deck anyway? Between the height of the deck and the fact it was built into the side of a hill, it wasn't exactly a head dive he wanted to take.

"So, this is Spence." The one checking the steaks glanced over his shoulder and nodded at him.

He knew not to take that as a welcome but more of a *yes, we see you*. Not exactly a threat but definitely not *not* a threat.

The man leaning against the railing nodded at Spence. "I'm Cam. The buffoon at the grill is Jamie."

At least they were trying to keep the tone light. Of course, that just meant he wouldn't see it coming when they killed him and buried him at sea.

Jamie looked at him over his shoulder and gave a nod. "You earned some points by bringing the beer. You should definitely stick with that plan for now."

Noah glanced at the table and asked, "Where's mine?"

"Well, here's the thing. You told me and Cam to pick up the steaks and potatoes. So we picked up steaks and potatoes.

You told us to let ourselves in. So we let ourselves in. You said to make ourselves at home. So we drank the beer."

Jamie flashed Noah a look that was completely unrepentant.

Spence started to relax. This wasn't going to be as bad as he feared when he'd seen the three huge guys lined up on the deck. The more they chatted, the more he felt like he was just hanging out as a guest at a new friend's house.

He tried to ignore any deeper implications.

It was bad enough that Noah could probably kill him with a paper straw before he knew anything was going on, but finding out Cam was a professional artesian who spent the day working wood with huge saws and Jamie basically ruled the Starlight Harbor version of the Seven Seas—diving over the railing if things went south was looking like a better option than he'd anticipated.

"Okay, enough shooting the bull. Time to get down to brass tacks."

Cam set his beer down and asked Jamie, "Could you fit a couple more clichés in there?"

"Just want to make sure we're on the same page." Jamie clapped his hands together with an evil grin. "Let's get down to this."

That did not bode well.

He might as well cut to the chase. They wouldn't be here if this wasn't about Lyra, so his suspicions must be right.

"I see how it is." Spence swept them all with the same glance. "Soften me up with steak and beer—beer I might add I bought—and then swoop in and finish me off."

"Here's the thing. Lyra's family, they're a little …" Cam shrugged as if Spence should be able to fill in the word himself.

When he didn't say anything, Jamie jumped in. "Crazy. Her family is nuts. Absolutely insane. And that's saying a lot for a family from Starlight Harbor. I mean, you already met Miss Angie."

Spence let his gaze travel to Noah to try to read his thoughts. It was great that Lyra had all these guys willing to look out for her, but that job seemed to fall to one of them specifically.

Noah had pushed his plate away and leaned back in his chair, crossing his arms over his chest and watching with an interest that Spence could only describe as rampant.

"I'm just here to make things right. I may not have been the one who did the damage, and Lyra already realizes she can't get on the Internet and say whatever she wants if it's attached to her name. But we can repair that and make sure she's safe from anyone who stumbles across references to that article."

"After what I saw earlier this evening," Noah speared him with a hard gaze, before continuing, "taking care of the damage done is the least of what we're talking about."

Yup. This is when he died.

Thirty was young, but he had lots of opportunities. It was his own fault for squandering them. He glanced at the railing again and shook it off.

He'd take it like a man.

Which, what did that even mean?

"Got it. Message received." Spence took a sip of his beer, shocked how disappointed he was that his suspicion was true.

Sure, he'd been talking himself out of his interest in Lyra all afternoon, but hearing that it was an absolute was a different thing. He ran through all the reasons why again—they were a bad match, he'd been her arch nemesis two days ago, he lived nowhere near here. Etcetera, etcetera.

But none of those seemed to matter as the gut punch he took when he looked at Noah.

"Wait a minute." Cam stared him down for a long moment before he started laughing. "Exactly what message do you think you're receiving?"

"About Noah and Lyra." Spence gave Noah his full attention. "Listen. I know what it looked like today when you got there, but if I had realized you two have been involved...or whatever is going on. Well, I'm not that kind of guy. I wouldn't pull that crap."

There was dead silence around the table, and Spence was pretty sure that was it.

While trying to come up with the right thing to diffuse the situation, the guys all glanced at one another and then back at him.

And then burst out laughing.

"Not in a million years," Jamie said. "Noah could only be so lucky."

"What?" Spence asked.

He glanced at Noah only to find the man blushing. Like straight up actually blushing right across his cheekbones.

He knew better than to laugh at a man for blushing.

"Lyra's like a little sister to me. To all of us, really." Noah shrugged like, *isn't she to everyone,* and continued. "We didn't date, we won't date, we aren't dating."

The relief was overwhelming.

"But that brings us to the next question." Noah leaned forward, bracing his elbows on the table, his hands lightly clasped in front of him. "What exactly are your intentions toward our Lyra?"

Oh boy.

Lyra

VIVIAN AND SKYE LAUGHED AT HER, BUT LYRA LOVED THE FIRST day when people arrived for a Christmas.

They were so excited and happy. They were all together with loved ones they hadn't seen in who knows how long.

Not to mention the sugar cookies. It was really fun to decorate the holiday cookies. Knowing there were fourteen kids in this group… Lyra was in heaven.

But she was also really, really far behind what with all the shenanigans happening yesterday.

Not to mention, she was working on no sleep. The almost-kiss in the lighthouse had kept her up all night. She nearly walked her butt over to pound on the door and demand Spence kiss her right then so she could get some sleep.

That probably wouldn't have done it.

She glanced at the clock wondering when her help was getting there. She usually had the Proctor twins come in and they weren't known for being late. Of course, there was still ten minutes till their shift, but they were usually so early Lyra had to get there early just to be ahead of them.

The best part of summer was she had their help on the Christmas weekdays when families arrived. Plus, she had a 50th anniversary cake that had to be done and decorated for tomorrow evening, which meant starting in… She looked at her watch again.

Now they were late. What was going on? It was an hour before opening though, so she started doing the chores she typically gave to them.

It was kind of relaxing doing all the basics. And again, decorating the sugar cookies. One of the best parts of the day. She'd rolled out and baked enough of them last night to decorate the first several batches while she had other things going.

But if she ever needed more than one set of hands, it was today.

Not only did she have all her fresh stuff to make and yesterday's cookies to frost, but she had a huge anniversary cake to bake.

It was so stinking exciting. The couple had met in Starlight Harbor fifty years ago when both families were celebrating the holiday—his because of his return, hers because of her brother's.

They'd become pen pals. *Pen pals.* So cute.

They wrote for three years before they finally realized that they needed to be together not apart.

And here's where it got hard. He was black. She was white. Fifty years ago wasn't one-hundred-and-fifty years ago, but it was still a challenge for some members in both families. She wished she could say today it wouldn't be for anyone.

But their love overcame that crap. Although the returning bride admitted they lost people in the long run, none were those closest to them.

To honor them finding one another here, she wanted this to be *perfect*.

But she had no idea how she was going to do the normal baking, run the shop, and get that cake and mini desserts done for tomorrow night if she didn't have help.

Dusting her hands off on her apron, she went in search of her personal cell phone to call the girls' mom. While she was up here, she might as well unlock the door. Almost no one came in before eight. The fishermen grabbed their coffee from Noah or down on the docks from Jamie. She was probably safe for another thirty minutes.

She seriously needed to get an earpiece so she didn't have to keep washing her hands, but she was unreasonably paranoid it would fall into something.

Finally, a breathless Mrs. Proctor answered the phone. "Hello?"

"Hi, Mrs. Proctor. It's Lyra. I was wondering if the girls are on their way."

"Oh. I didn't even think to call you." She rushed on before Lyra could jump in. "The girls are with their father this week."

"But…" Lyra wasn't sure what to say that wasn't blowing her already worried top. "They both confirmed they'd work today. We have a big order, and I need their hands."

"Well, their father offered to bring them with him to Boston this weekend, and since it's just your little cookie store, I let them so I don't have to deal with his lawyer this week. They left this morning. Just walked out the door about twenty minutes ago."

Lyra waited, because surely there was more to it than that.

When nothing came she took a deep breath and said, "I'm all alone here and shorthanded now. When will they be back?"

"I *said* they were gone for the weekend. Maybe you shouldn't rely on high school girls to run your business."

"Well, you can let them know that after being no-shows and their mother being rude and irresponsible, I won't."

Lyra hung up before she could get another word in.

Lyra had never liked that woman but had hired her daughters because she felt bad for them. This is what you get for having a soft heart, she told herself. Walked all over.

And yes, she knew she shouldn't call any woman, especially one of her elders "that woman." But, she totally was.

In her head, that is.

The twins have been upfront about the fact that they needed to make money for college because their parents kept fighting over who was going to pay for it. Of course, Mrs. Proctor would probably say that's what lawyers were for.

But when Lyra hadn't had an option, she took the twins. While what they told Spence was true—Starlight Harbor wasn't a dying town—it was small, and did have its struggles.

With the twins, if you took one you took them both. And Lyra's thinking had been that if one was sick, the other would be here.

Apparently, not so much.

The fact they'd chosen to go and didn't call was the death ring for their coffin. Forget the nails—that puppy was welded shut.

"Hey. These muffins look amazing."

Lyra nearly jumped out of her skin, barely holding onto the phone she was still glaring at.

"I didn't hear you come in." She ran a hand down the front of her apron, dusting it off and making sure she wasn't a complete mess already.

"I'm not surprised." Spence laughed and gave her a big smile. "You apparently had something to say to someone."

Lyra wasn't the type of person to tell someone off, so she definitely wasn't the type of person to get caught doing it.

"Her two daughters work for me on busy weeks. And they both decided to just not. And she doesn't seem to have a problem with that."

Spence let out a low whistle. "My mother would kick my butt all the way up to the point and back again."

Lyra wasn't sure what her mother would do. Probably tell her to follow her bliss. Then again, Lyra wouldn't have left someone in the lurch like that.

"So you called in your backup?"

She started laughing because...well, she needed that.

"This is Starlight Harbor on a Christmas arrival day—there is no backup. All hands on deck, and all that." She slid the muffin he'd been eyeing onto a plate and carried it to the counter. "Coffee?"

"Sure."

She listed the day's brews and grinned when she was done. "Or, regular?"

"That would be great."

"Consider it an acceptable bribe for the new article. You can't review what you haven't tasted."

He wanted to argue. Instead he dropped a ten in the tip jar when she wasn't looking.

This small town business thing was a whole 'nother world to him. It was kind of fascinating.

"What happens now?" he asked.

"Recover." She glanced around behind the counter, taking a broad sweep of everything.

She could do this. It wasn't like she was being judged—well, besides by the customers, the anniversary party, and Spence—but if she blocked that all out, she could totally do this. She grabbed her notebooks and a cup of tea, came around the counter, and sat down at the table closest to the kitchen door, unsurprised when Spence joined her.

Lyra opened her main notebook and pulled out the pages for today so she could look at them all at once. She had her laminated Christmas arrival day list, her catered party list, and her daily list.

"That's a lot of checkboxes," Spence said as he glanced over her pages.

"Checkboxes make the world go 'round." She flashed him a grin. "So now, Mr. How Do Small Town Businesses Run, we start sorting by necessity. I've already got sugar cookies baked but they need to be frosted."

She pulled out a notebook from the stack and flipped forward a couple pages.

"Here's the standard cookies we do for Christmas week. There are twenty-two different types of frosted sugar cookies."

Yesterday she baked seven sheets.

The old handwritten directions she'd done when she first started stood out next to the photos. Each one was intricately decorated with balls and piping.

"Those are not cookies." Spence looked up at her, a deep appreciation she could see clearly in his eyes. "Those are works of art, and if I bought one I'd be afraid to eat it."

"Trust me, seven-year-olds have no qualms eating these cookies." She glanced through the pages, wondering if she'd done enough. "I made enough for today and probably tomorrow, but frosting them is going to take time. That goes in the necessity column; baking more today goes in the review column."

Sorting the stickies went on opposite sides of the table as Spence gave her what she could only call a goofy grin.

"I'm about a million miles over my head already." Spence watched as she did the same thing for her daily list, then worked through her Christmas list, then looked at the anniversary party.

"The party is where I can't skimp. It has to be a homerun. It's a big deal for these people. I don't want to be the person who lets them down. I want to be the person who makes it a night to remember."

When they started, she'd been a little more hopeful, but looking at all the Post-Its still on the right side of the table, not so much. Trying to keep a hopeful look on her face and an optimistic idea in her heart, Lyra tried to figure out how she was going to pull this off.

"So, where do we get started?"

She froze, looking up at the man who had nearly bank-rupted her business now offering to help her save the day.

"Um, so…" Of course, saving the day was easier when you actually could bake. "Not to look a gift horse in the mouth or anything, but can you bake?"

Spence grinned and shrugged a bit. "Not a lot. But I'm a great extra pair of hands. Plus I can keep the front clean, ring up people, help them with their order, pour tea. If you say 'pull that out of the oven,' I'll remember to put on those big mittens first so we don't have to go to the hospital."

She still wasn't sure what to do with him. There was no time to train someone to do anything, but the way he made it sound he'd just do things that took common sense.

If only she could be sure he had common sense to spare.

"It can't hurt, right?" He glanced down at the stickies again. "I'm sure there's something you could teach me to do that would keep me out of the way and let you get important stuff done. It would be fun to work together for a day."

It was true. She needed to get all of the Post-Its that were left done. There wasn't really any option in that.

"Okay, let's start with the register. It's super easy. I use Square."

She walked him through that and talked him through the first two sales for morning coffee and muffins as she frosted the first set of cookies to get them ready for decorating.

"Got it." Spence handed the woman her to-go cup and turned back to Lyra. "What's next on the flash training schedule?"

Lyra glanced at the list and wondered what she could give him.

"The locals will start coming in for real now, so you're going to be completely in charge of the front. Make sure we have coffee at all times or there will be a revolt and I won't feel bad using you as a human shield."

"Coffee. Got it."

"If you could pull everything on the list that's clipped to the front of the walk-in for the banana bread and custard tarts while I finish this, that would be great."

"Not a problem."

He started out back, but when the chime over the door sounded he beelined to the counter, put the woman's order together, rung her up, and then carried on.

He was more efficient than two teens with cell phones any day.

He lifted. He carried. He fetched. He cleaned. He put away.

It was heaven. And, in the meantime, he asked questions. Tons and tons of questions.

Why the bakery? Where did she study? What was her favorite thing to make? Why did she come back to Starlight Harbor? What was her best seller? What did she exclusively make when Christmas guests were here? How often did she have events like the engagement party? Did she ever close the shop? What was she going to do now that the twins were out?

She got enough cookies decorated to put on display and to send the daily cookie tray over to Noah.

"What's up with the cookie tray?" Spence asked, carrying on the question brigade.

"He doesn't want to have to make desserts and the older gentlemen who hang out there in the afternoon like cookies. He also puts in orders for actual desserts every three days."

Thank goodness today wasn't one of those days.

Of course, Noah would probably just toss some premade dough in his oven and call it good.

The morning crowd slowed down and gave Lyra time to focus on the plan for the engagement party. She was halfway through the petit fours when she heard the chime of the front door and noticed how quiet it had been.

Glancing at the clock, she was shocked to see it was after lunch.

"Hey." Spence came through the front door, a bag in hand. "Chicken salad on croissants, made by the talented baker across the square, and some sweet potato chips."

He set the bag down and started unpacking it, leaving Lyra to finish what she was on and take her work apron off.

"How's it going?" he asked as she carried two iced teas over and tossed the gross packets of fake sugar he seemed to like at him.

She was going to have to work on his taste palate if that's what he was putting in her unflavored teas.

"Good." She took a bite of the sandwich, judging how her croissant had held up. She made them yesterday and was pleased with the taste and texture. Watching as Spence bit into his and the happy look on his face, she went on. "I've been surprised how quiet it is. The families must be arriving later than usual."

"Why's that?" he asked as he popped a chip in his mouth.

"Because we're usually overrun with people wanting an afternoon snack after they're settled."

"Oh." Spence glanced out the window then back at her before taking another bite of his sandwich. "How's the cake and stuff coming?"

Lyra opened her mouth before she realized she'd been diverted.

"What's going on?"

Spence pointed to his mouth and kept chewing. After a moment, she had to wonder what exactly he was chewing.

"Spence. What are you not telling me?"

He took a sip of tea—either to wash down the chicken salad or to stall longer.

When he couldn't put it off any more, Spence set his glass down and reached across the table to take her hand.

"Oh, that's not good." Lyra looked at her hand in his. "Just tell me straight."

Spence glanced over her shoulder again and out the window. She knew what was coming. She didn't like it, but maybe it wasn't as bad as she thought.

"The guests are here. Most of the families with kids arrived before lunch and ate down at the restaurant on the water."

She nodded.

This was new. Especially with kids. She was used to being overrun as the special vacation treat.

And no one had come in.

Lyra stood and tossed her napkin on the table, determined to get to the bottom of this. She stepped out of the bakery, into the bright midday sun surprise to see just how right Spence was.

There were people everywhere.

That wasn't uncommon for a Christmas week. The

surrounding towns knew the schedule and came in for the festivities and special events.

And usually for her cookies.

But not today. The bakery was empty, and while she had been thankful for the quiet as she prepped for the party, she couldn't help but be surprised by just how bad business was.

She waited until an unfamiliar face was walking by and stopped them.

"Hey, have you tried the bakery?"

The woman shook her head and glanced in the window. "No. We read on the way up all the reviews on the tourism site, and that was the only shop they said to steer clear of. Kind of sad it's right here on the square, huh?"

Lyra gave her a tight smile as the family walked away.

She glanced around the square, watching people mill about everywhere, and realized that things were far worse than she thought.

"Oh, Cupcake." Spence stood behind her holding the door open. "I'm so sorry. I thought that was taken care of."

She pushed back the tears she didn't want him to see. Not because she didn't want him to feel guilty, because part of her did. But because she absolutely was not going to let him think this could beat her.

Shoulders set, she brushed by him back into the store, determined to make the most of the day.

No matter what was going on, she still had a really important party tomorrow that she absolutely did not want to let down.

Maybe this was one of those silver lining things—plenty of free time to get caught up without the girls here.

She'd deal with the Yelp thing later.

Before she could get back to work, someone cleared his throat at the counter. Spence stood on the other side of the counter.

"Did you want to take off?"

She wouldn't blame him. He probably had plenty of things to do, and now that there wasn't a lot he could get done here, he might as well take off.

"Not exactly. But I'd like to buy two dozen cookies."

"I don't need your pity purchase."

"It's not a pity purchase." Spence took his wallet out and put it down in front of him. "I have things to do with these. There's a cookie emergency," he said, quoting Noah from the day before.

"What is with you guys and cookie emergencies?"

"So am I going to get those cookies or not?" Spence slid down so he could look into the pastry display. "I'd like an assortment of two dozen of the holiday sugar cookies. Just for good measure, could I have one more dozen unfrosted, please?"

"Unfrosted?"

"Yes. Unfrosted."

"You want to bring my cookies, unfrosted, with no decorations, out to the world for your cookie emergency?" Lyra crossed her arms over her chest.

"Not everyone likes that much sugar."

Lyra sucked in a breath and tried not to gasp.

"These are not all sugar."

"They are literally called sugar cookies."

"That's not my point. These cookies have the perfect balance of cookie to frosting ratio. To get them unfrosted would be…" She didn't even know what to say to that.

"You know, some people would like to enjoy your cookies as they would like them. Like those people who get headaches from too much natural sugar."

Spence glanced away, his jaw tightening just a bit.

"Is that why you put that fake stuff in your tea? "

Spence gave a sharp nod.

"Sugar can trigger my migraines if I'm not careful," he admitted reluctantly. "It's stupid to let a little headache slow you down."

"Who called your migraines little headaches?" Because she was going to destroy that person.

Like, for real. Not just threaten to destroy them, then meet them and want to kiss them destroy-them.

"Just...someone."

She was betting someone was an ex.

Well, exes were exes for a reason.

Lyra glanced around, quickly trying to figure out what to do.

"You can be around it, though, right? It's not like peanuts or perfume, right?"

"No. No, absolutely not." He reassured her as quickly as possible. "It's just... Well, I'd kind of like some of your cookies. And I have some people I need to share them with."

She couldn't shake the feeling he was up to something, but even if it was just to go hang out with Noah and the guys at the café since nothing was going on here, she couldn't really blame him.

"Okay. Two dozen frosted, one unfrosted."

She tried not to panic since he looked like he'd just won something and she wasn't sure what. Either way, she didn't have the time to figure out what he was up to. She had to stay on her schedule.

He insisted on paying for his cookies, then marched out of the bakery, obviously on a mission.

It was surprisingly quiet without him there.

Not that she missed him or anything.

Okay, she totally missed him.

Spence

"I NEED A TRAY." SPENCE DIDN'T WAIT FOR THE LINE IN FRONT of him to make way. He just walked right behind Noah's counter as if he belonged there.

"Good to see you, too. I'm a little busy, what with lunch service and all, but make yourself at home." The last was obviously high on the sarcasm scale.

"Right. Lyra is going under. The Yelp page isn't down. No one has gone in. I have cookies to pimp but no tray."

Noah slid a glance his way. It was something between exasperation and acceptance.

"I have a few I need to return to her. Take your pick in the stack drawer to the right of the sink."

Spence had no idea what that meant and was beginning to realize he needed to learn what went on in kitchens if he was going to level up in the adulting world.

He doubled down on this when he set up the tray and it looked like an eight-year-old did it.

He was just going to go with good intentions and an attempt at charm and head out the door.

"Hey, Spence."

Spence turned back toward Noah just in time to get hit in the face with the Santa hat he threw at him.

"'Tis the season, man. Christmas week. Christmas cookies. Christmas hat." Noah laughed as Spence put the tray down and stuck the hat on his head.

The hat matched the mission. Ridiculous or not.

The first group of people he saw was mulling around outside the gifts and paper shop. Spence gave them the once-over. Comfortable shoes, oversize bags, big-rimmed hats and glasses.

Definitely tourists.

And, their hats were even brighter than his—a purple and a red one.

"Ladies, can I offer you some Christmas cookies?" Spence put on his most charming smile, which as a nerd boy who worked online was questionable at best.

Darn it, he should've called Cam. That pretty boy would get anyone eating out of the palm of his hands.

Or Jamie… He'd swagger on over and probably walk away with as many dates as cookies that he gave away.

Geez, even Noah had more game than he did. Noah would just glare—or as the girls put it, smolder—and look all tough and be like, "Cookies, ladies?" in that gravelly military voice, and they would probably swoon before taking the cookies.

He thought they were just going to look at him with his tray of cookies and his stupid hat and walk away. Instead, they came closer to check out the different designs.

"These are gorgeous." The Purple Hat raised her cell phone to take a picture. When he realized he was in the frame, Spence gave an uncomfortable smile. He had not signed up for this.

Or, maybe he had when he'd driven eight hours to try to fix the chaos he created.

She took a couple more shots of the cookies and then picked one up and a bit into it.

"I didn't expect them to taste as good as they look."

"I'm not sure I want to eat my favorite one. It's so pretty I'd feel guilty." She shook her red-hatted head. "I should pick my least favorite."

"You have a least favorite?" her friend asked.

"Right. I'll have the snowman." She picked it up and took a bite. "Wow. Delicious. This is what we should bring everyone back as gifts."

Things would turn around if everything went like this. All he had to do was get out on the street and make people realize how awesome Lyra's stuff was.

"Where are these from?"

"They're from The Sweetest Things." Spence turned to point across the square at Lyra's to shop, only to see her striding across the green. "Here comes the owner now."

One of the women leaned in and lowered her voice. "This can't be hers. We saw her reviews on the tourism site and checked Yelp too."

Spence cringed at the statement. It was one thing to suspect you might be the reason for a slow day. It was another thing to hear you basically torpedoed the nicest woman in the world's business.

"Yup. We're aware of the situation. If you noticed, they all came in on one day. Lyra was hit by a bunch of trolls because of a Santa-hat-wearing idiot's guide to small towns."

Lyra sidled up beside him, glancing up at the hat and then down at the tray.

"Spence, what exactly are you doing?"

"Um, trying to repair the damage done by my idiots?" Even he heard it as a question, not a statement.

He motioned toward the women next to him. "These lovely ladies think the cookies are works of art."

"So, let me get this straight." Purple Hat glanced between them. "Some Santa-hat-wearing idiot—that would be him—sandbagged your bakery and now is trying to fix it?"

Lyra's eyes rolled toward the heavens, as if she thought help might come from the clouds on a rainbow wave of crème brûlée.

"That would be the short version. Although, I had no idea he was out here with cookies trying to force them on people and harassing visitors."

"This cutie?" Red Hat glanced at Spence, and he was suddenly afraid she was going to pat him on the behind. "He could never harass anyone."

Lyra mumbled something under her breath he was pretty sure was *yeah right.*

"I don't think anyone walking around giving out delicious cookies could be considered a harasser." The second woman looked at them again and smiled in what could only be called a coquettish way. "I don't suppose I could have a snowflake, too?"

"For you? A snowflake." Spence held out the tray and she took another cookie. "But, you're missing out. Lyra has an assortment of different cookies over there, along with muffins, cupcakes, custards, everything. She's pretty amazing. You should see the nine-level chocolate raspberry cake she made the other day."

He started to pull his phone out of his back pocket but stopped when Lyra shook her head, obviously embarrassed by his show of pride.

"Layer." Lyra tried not to laugh. "Not level, layer."

"What's the difference?" Spence looked down at her, amazed again at how incredibly beautiful she was. Just adorably so. Focused and passionate about her work. The freckles, the bright-green eyes. Even the way her hair blew in the wind...not like normal hair. Like angel-slash-elf hair. She was—

Crap, she was talking again.

He zoomed back in on the conversation.

"One happens in buildings, one happens in pastries."

"Right." Spence glanced up their audience and grinned. "See? Pastry genius."

Next to him, Lyra gave out a deep groan.

"I have to get back to work." She turned toward the two ladies and smiled. "Thank you for the kind words about the cookies. I'm really glad you liked them. I hope you enjoy Starlight Harbor."

And with that she turned and headed off across the green, still shaking her head at Spence as she went.

"You're not going to let that girl get away, are you?"

Spence turned back when he realized he'd been watching Lyra the entire time she crossed both streets and the green between them.

"You mean, right now?" he asked as Lyra's door fell shut behind her.

"You really are a Santa-hat-wearing idiot, aren't you?"

"It's this younger generation. They just have no common sense."

"Shortsighted. Can't see what's right in front of them."

"But I can see you have a good heart with how you're out here giving away cookies."

Purple Hat gave him a hard glance. "How did you get these cookies?"

Spence had been watching the conversation like a tennis match he didn't know who to root for. "I bought them. I swear. Even left money in the tip jar."

Red Hat reached up and patted him on the cheek. "Excellent, we'll spread the word about the bakery. Don't be an idiot." And with that, the two women sauntered off into the gift store probably continuing to judge him.

But they were right about one thing.

He was beginning to think he couldn't let Lyra get away.

19

Lyra

"Did you know there's a vagrant walking the streets of Starlight Harbor, forcing visitors to eat cookies and praise The Sweetest Things?" She tried not to growl into her phone.

Lyra wasn't sure what she was so angry about, but boy, was she mad.

There he was, out there swaying over women with his appeal and charm to go spend their money in her shop.

Well, it was no better than when men hired hot women in bikinis to stand in front of cars.

Her cookies didn't need Mr. Hottie Pants pimping them to be worth buying.

"By *vagrant*, you mean…?" Skye's voice was way too calm over the phone for this dire situation.

"I mean a person with no local address."

"Perhaps the one staying with Noah?"

"Is he? Is he staying with Noah? Or was Noah forced to take him in like a house arrest kind of thing?" She could hear the hysteria rising in her voice and didn't care.

He had to be stopped.

"From what?" Skye asked.

Apparently she'd been having that hysteria out loud.

Darn it.

"From...from..."

"Okay, honey, why don't you take a deep breath. I've got Vi with me—"

"Why do you have Vivian with you?"

"We're going to lunch."

"Without me?" Lyra squeaked.

"Um, no. We were on our way to pick up lunch and bring it to you. But if we'd known you'd scheduled a full-blown breakdown for today, we would have been there sooner."

Lyra glanced out her window. Instead of spotting Skye's Jeep, she just saw Spence leaning over to let a little kid take a cookie and straighten his Santa hat.

Curse him and his adorableness, that mob boss instigator!

While she glared out the window, the Jeep pulled into view, and Vivian sat in the front seat looking at her like she was insane while Skye answered her walkie.

She kept working on the quiches that would be used for the opening of the party tomorrow and frowned over her counter.

They were out there talking about her. She knew it. This wasn't paranoia at all.

Vivian said something, and Skye burst out laughing.

See? Laughing at her.

They both slid out of the Jeep and came in, Vivian carrying a large pizza box from the local pub.

"Hey." Vivian set the pizza down and grabbed some napkins, stopping when she noticed the glare Lyra was giving her. "What's with the death stare?"

"You're talking about me."

Vivian gave her a long look and shook her head, walking back to the pizza.

"One, not everything is about you. I was talking about

Tyler's first crush. But if you see a parallel, that's all you. Two, I have forty-five minutes, so get your butt over here to discuss this 'emergency' of yours before I have to get back to the garage for when Tyler gets out of baseball camp."

"Right." Lyra sat down with a huff, still trying to figure out this new angry streak she had. "So, what are you going to do about this vagrant?"

"Lyra, you know—"

"Hi there! It's us." The two older ladies with the big hats came into the shop. "Now that your young man is out there clearing your name, we thought we should get here early to do our gift orders."

"Right," Purple Hat added. "He's really working up some business. Such a sweet boy."

"Uh-huh."

"Anyway, I'd like to order three boxes of one dozen Christmas cookies. I'm bringing them back to my bingo ladies so they know I thought of them while I was here."

"She thought of them because she set a reminder in her phone."

"So, I still thought of them."

Lyra couldn't help but smile as she listened to the two women banter. She gave them their option of the holiday, the seaside, or the lighthouse box to put each in, added the orders to her calendar, and rang them up.

"I'm sure you'll be plenty busy by the time he gets all the way around the square. And we're telling everyone to ignore those reviews from those bullies."

"Thank you so much." Lyra smiled, afraid it might shatter if she didn't get to decompress soon.

"We'll see you tomorrow night. I'll be first in line for that cake!"

When she was finally able to sit down with her girls, Lyra

glanced between them, knowing they were coming to the same conclusion she was.

She was nuts.

"What is going on with you?" Vivian stuck a piece of pizza in her mouth, obviously having said everything she needed to.

Skye just sat there, watching her carefully, wondering where this was going. Not at all surprising, since that's how she spent most of her day.

"I don't know. I'm really, really angry. But also, really not angry. Like distracted by how adorable everything is. But also angry at it."

Vivian nodded her head. "Yup, I hear you. There's nothing you can do about it."

Skye glanced between them. "Are you sure? Seems like there should be a way out of this."

"Nope." Vi shook her head. "I think it's a done deal. She's just going to have to face facts."

"Just have to deal with what?"

Vivian snorted and Skye stuffed another piece of pizza in her mouth, obviously not wanting to be the one to share the bad news.

"Well?"

"I'm not going to dance around this anymore. It ain't pretty." Vivian put both her hands on the table and leaned forward, meeting Lyra eye to eye. "You're falling for this guy. No way around it."

Lyra collapsed back in her chair.

"No. Absolutely not that."

"The driving halfway across the country—"

"A couple hours."

"To rescue you—"

"Fix what he screwed up."

"Sticking around to make it better—"

115

"Because I threatened to sue him." Lyra smirked as she added, "And because I apparently have a bodyguard named Noah."

"The whole almost kissing you in the lighthouse." Vivian fanned herself. "Very romantic. Only you could get yourself almost kissed in a former prison."

"Jail." Skye jumped in. "Technically, a prison is—"

"Nobody cares." Vivian shook her head at Skye to shut that down before going on, "Then coming in to help when your teens bailed on you—which, bad form. Just an FYI, Mrs. Proctor goes to the bottom of the oil change list since she always tries to push herself in last minute."

"Um, thanks?" Lyra was all for girl solidarity, but Vivian actually came at that in very different ways sometimes.

"So, he finds out you're still getting bombed by the Yelp page—"

"Which is technically his fault."

"Which is technically the people's fault who went on there and killed your rating."

"Which they wouldn't do if he hadn't written that article."

Vivian sighed, obviously unsure how to phrase this in a way that Lyra would hear, but powered on.

"Lyra, honey, he'd posted that article three times before and no one ever attacked anyone. Not only that, but the town never even heard about it."

"Are you saying this is my fault? That I brought this on myself? That I deserve it?"

She was ready to stand up and throw her best friends out, but Vivian was shaking her head. "No one deserves to get treated like this. But, and I'm going to agree with Noah on this one, you walked into a situation where you didn't know the community or culture and broke both of them."

"Noah said that?" Skye's brows came down as she glanced between them.

"No. He said she went in without proper intel."

Skye rolled her eyes. "Of course he did."

Both women went back to their pizza, letting Lyra mull.

"I can't be in love with him. I just met him."

"I didn't say you were in love with him." Vivian shook her head, giving Lyra an encouraging smile. "Not everyone we start to fall for do we actually fall in love with. But, this is Starlight Harbor. We're the capital of finding your soul mate. Think of all those people who've only been here for a weekend to come back for their weddings, anniversaries, to bring their children. It's not a coincidence we've gained the slogan Love Happens Here."

"So what do I do?" Lyra had always expected to find the right guy to fall for, to fall all the way for.

Heck, she'd lived in Starlight Harbor her whole life, and Vivian was right. They saw people fall in love on the turn of a heartbeat nearly every weekend. It was like the air and the water and the magic all came together here, and BAM!

And she'd waited...and waited. But didn't find the guy who made her a mushy mess.

Now that she was a mushy mess, she didn't think she cared for it.

It was very disconcerting.

"He doesn't live here, he has no reason to move here, he nearly bankrupted my business, and there's no way he feels the same."

Skye rolled her eyes. "Seriously?"

"What she's trying to say," Vivian jumped in with a look at Skye, "is that how do you know he doesn't feel the same?"

Lyra's mind rushed through it all. Because he hadn't shown anything beyond a need to fix the mess he created. Because he had had the chance to kiss her and had passed? Because he—

"Okay, stop." Vivian shook her head.

117

"What?"

Skye laughed. "Honey, we can all but see the cartoon thought bubbles over your head coming up with everything from he didn't kiss you to you suspect he might like puppies more than kittens and that suddenly became a deal breaker for you."

Lyra narrowed her eyes. The puppies-kitten thing was beyond too much even for them.

"I never thought you were a coward." Vivian took another sip of tea, looking for all the world that she hadn't just thrown down some fighting words.

"I'm not." Lyra looked from one friend to the next, the panic subsiding and forming into something different, something new.

She wasn't going to let a little fear stop her from something that might be the best thing that could happen to her. It's true, she was afraid. Why didn't people talk about the absolute terror that came along with the question of love?

"I'm not a coward." She balled her hands into fists and took a deep breath. "I'm not a coward, I'm a daredevil."

20

Spence

HE WAS OUT OF COOKIES.

He took the time to go back to The Sweetest Things and check in to see if Lyra had started to get the business he'd been sending her way for the last hour. Hopefully his efforts had been worth the while.

And, he'd managed to only have three of the unfrosted cookies.

At the door, he glanced in and saw her rushing from one order to the next, a line of four small groups at the counter.

She'd never make the schedule for the engagement party tomorrow. Not without his help. Maybe he'd overdone it?

He swung through the door, focused on helping her. It seemed like a small dragon to slay, but still—everyone's dragon is different.

"I'm back." He came around the counter, grabbing a red apron to match the hat he was still wearing. "Sorry I was gone so long."

"Right." She flashed him a smile. "Cookie emergency."

She nodded at the sink, a reminder for the non-baker to wash his hands before he got to work.

"Take off, baker girl. I've got this."

He tried not to grin too much as he took over the counter.

"Merry Christmas, ladies. What delicious thing can I get you today?"

While she worked in the kitchen, he bantered with the guests, asking where they were from, about their visit, all the things that made them feel welcome.

It was as if he'd been here forever—and only a minute.

He closed his eyes for a second and tried to picture his life back in New York. It wasn't a bad life. He had guys he played softball with every Saturday, his parents had been nearby before they retired, he dated off and on but nothing serious.

Most of his college friends were still down in the city and were beginning to drift to occasional Facebook posts and invites to weddings.

Like he said, not a bad life.

But not an inspiring one, either. Not one he'd fight to keep.

He smiled as another family came in with small children.

"Merry Christmas!" He leaned, watching them pick their treat while the parents talked about their plans for the weekend.

Apparently they were in town for the man's brother's return from overseas. He was showing up tomorrow, and they had the two cottages he'd loved so much down by the water.

"Great view, right?" Spence asked.

"Amazing. We can't get over how cute this place is." He leaned against the counter as his wife wandered around looking at all the cute bakery-themed things Lyra had decorated the shop with. "I was expecting something really tacky, you know?"

Spence felt himself tighten, trying not to show annoyance

before he realized he was this guy. Making assumptions about super cute towns without having seen them.

No wonder he'd failed to become a travel journalist. It wasn't that he'd gotten himself locked in and in debt—although that certainly didn't help him get where he'd wanted to be. Somewhere along the line he'd forgotten why he was passionate about travel and journalism, let alone the combination of the two.

He hadn't felt that way in Starlight Harbor.

He'd been refreshed and excited about everything. Everywhere he looked was a potential article.

Had his single-mindedness gotten attached to the wrong path?

Or was it Lyra? Was she the thing that reignited his passion and had him dying to write again?

All he knew was he had to get *Roadside Adventures* back on track so he could sell it and move on. Hopefully he'd get himself as far out of debt as possible. Maybe he could find a way to home base here. He probably didn't even need that much of a storage unit. The stuff back at his place was feeling more and more like an anchor instead of a home.

Also, no offense IKEA and Walmart, but they'd be there with dressers and side tables when he needed them again.

He shook his head as he did a loop around the café, wiping the tables down and clearing off the bus tray full of used cups and plates.

It all hinged on being able to sell the website. He'd put nearly a decade into this thing and he needed to get ahead of his bills enough to be able to eat.

But, this opportunity to write about something really great, to show people there was more to short-term vacation spots—it was an amazing idea.

There was so much here in the US people overlooked and

he had the chance to make the best disregarded places really shine.

Sure, he loved going on safari as much as the next guy. But there were people focused on sharing those stories and making sure those places had the attention they needed.

Most Americans would never see them. But he was shocked how many people didn't know what was in their own backyard. Almost literally sometimes.

There was something about the idea of spotlighting those that made his brain kick into overdrive.

Lyra brushed her hands down her apron and looked over the empty case.

"We might as well close. You've sold everything and then some." She did a sweep of the room as he wiped down the tables. "I'm not sure how you got that many to-go orders for the end of the weekend. I'll be up Saturday night."

"Oh, I didn't think of that."

Of course he didn't. He was too focused on making up for the lost sales. But she'd been working the back by herself all day.

He needed to get past the obvious numbers. Total rookie mistake.

Kind of like assuming Starlight Harbor was a Tiny Tacky Town.

"What can I do to help?" he asked as he finished the tables and grabbed the broom.

"Actually," she came around the counter as she took off her apron. "It's kind of a blessing in disguise. I never get to go to the Christmas parade."

Spence's head came up, surprised at the news.

"There's a parade?"

That definitely would have gotten his attention. He wasn't a parade addict or anything, but he never understood people who didn't enjoy a good parade.

"Yup. Thursday evenings every time we have a Christmas."

He wasn't trying to get excited. It was just happening naturally.

"So… Is there a Santa Claus?"

She shook her head as much out of obvious frustration as amusement. "You really did absolutely no research on Starlight Harbor, did you?"

It was getting more than just obvious. It was getting embarrassing.

"I think we can all admit I saw Christmas year round and kicked into high stupidity gear. Let's just accept that as a given and move on. Tell me about the Santa parade."

She gave him a look and he realized he was bouncing on his toes.

"Man, you really love parades."

"Are there people who don't?"

"Yes. All over the world. And even most people just *like* parades. Not like this. I mean people like parades, but I don't think I've ever seen anyone over the age of six love a parade like you do."

"I take it it's not a big deal here then?"

"Oh no. It's a big deal. It's huge actually." She gave a smile that told him she was half informing, half humoring him. "And yes, there is a Santa Claus."

Spence all but pumped his fist in the air.

"I knew it. So when does this Christmas parade with Santa happen?"

"A bit after dinner. We try to keep it early enough for the little kids to enjoy it but late enough that the lights on the sleigh and other floats can really be seen."

She started laughing before he opened his mouth and he had a feeling that his face was saying everything he wanted to say already.

123

"There's a sleigh? Like, a real sleigh?"

"Kind of. There is a wooden sleigh built over an old motorized frame. It's been around since the 40s. Some really famous wood artist made it, but you have to ask Cam about that. He's the expert."

Spence tried to ratchet his excitement down because it was just a sleigh and he didn't want to look like a thirty-year-old idiot.

Well, more than he had for the last couple of days.

She went back to the kitchen and he could hear her putting the last of her tools away as he took the drawer out and counted it down to fifty dollars as she instructed.

Lyra came back out and swept a look over the room. "I feel like there should be more to do. At least we know you're worth more than two teenage girls, that's for sure."

"Glad to hear I'm worth anything in your eyes at this point."

"Let's just say, it's still touch and go."

Spence puttered around while she finished all her end of the day stuff.

Maybe he could get her to go to the parade with him.

She said she never got to go, so maybe she'd appreciate the invite. But maybe she'd like to spend it with her friends. Or she was sick of him. She was probably sick of him before she even met him. Maybe she just didn't want to share the parade with him.

Look at what happened when she shared her lighthouse. Locked in the jail.

But, he wouldn't know if he didn't try, and this girl was worth stepping out on that ledge for.

"Hey—"

"Do you want to go to the parade with me tonight?" Lyra asked before he could finish his question.

"Oh." She'd beaten him to it and now he couldn't get his mind to catch back up.

Maybe she just wanted to keep working on his tour of the town. He'd missed the opportunity to show her he wanted to take her to the parade. Not just hanging out.

Was he being an idiot? He didn't think so. He was falling for this girl faster than he was falling for the town. And that was saying something.

"I mean," she hurried on, "you don't have to. No pressure. I mean…"

"No, it's not that." He crossed the room and took both her hands, needing to touch her so she could feel how much he wanted to be near her, to spend time with her. "I was about to ask you and you beat me to it. I would love to go to the parade. And I would especially love to go with you."

He rocked back on his heels, feeling especially proud of himself as that little blush that raced across her freckle-covered nose came out.

"Great." Lyra smiled up at him and the room froze in time. It could be winter outside for all he knew at this point. "Really, that sounds great."

They made arrangements, agreeing when he should come by and pick her up. And he felt like he was seventeen all over again. Like any moment it could all fall apart or her parents would bust in and say, *absolutely not, this boy is trouble*.

Instead, he waited as she locked up and watched her stride around to the stairs that went up the side of the building to her little apartment above the bakery.

He couldn't help but wonder what it was like to always smell all her great concoctions, or if she was immune to it.

He didn't think you'd ever become immune to anything that had to do with her.

Lyra

SHE SHOULD CHANGE. SHE SHOULD ABSOLUTELY CHANGE. She'd been wearing these clothes all day.

But what if Spence read more into her changing than she meant it to be?

Of course, she didn't know what she meant it to be, so there was that.

She got in the shower and washed the day off—a combination of sugar and sweat that always seemed to take an extra rinse to get rid of—thinking about how it had started as such a mess and turned out so great. Even having been shorthanded, leaving her with Spence there all day, turned out to be a big silver lining.

And now she got to go to the parade.

Usually she kept the shop open because there were always people who avoided the crowd, getting some much needed alone time, or who read while sipping tea and eating snacks.

And, since that was her gig, she was typically thankful. But just for once it was nice to get to go enjoy herself and not worry about making sure others were happy.

She was standing in front of her closet, contemplating

which dress stated most clearly "I'm not expecting this to be a date, but I hope it is, but don't read into the fact that I hope it is" when there was a knock on the door.

She glanced at her clock with a bit of panic before realizing it was nearly three hours before Spence was supposed to come by to pick her up.

Pulling on her light summer bathrobe, she strode to the foyer to deal with whoever was there to ruin her chill time.

"Open up. It's us." Skye's voice came through the door, apparently annoyed it wasn't open yet.

It's not like she didn't have a key. Or that the door was even locked.

"Come on in," Lyra shouted as she turned back into her room. "I'm getting ready."

She was getting ready several hours early, but who could blame her? She hadn't been on a date since—

Well, years. Not since she studied in Paris probably.

Occasionally, one of the guests would ask her out. But none that appealed to her enough to deal with the discomfort of dating someone in town just for a few days.

She paused in brushing her hair as she realized that that was exactly what she was doing.

Spence could be gone any second, but she was glad she was going out with him tonight.

"Wash the fairy dust off?" Vivian glanced around her very girly bathroom.

Lyra was unashamed of the lotions and hair clips and lip glosses that cluttered the counter. Everyone embraced their femininity differently.

That didn't mean she didn't know what was coming next.

"I don't even know what to do with half the stuff in your bathroom." Vivian laughed at her own self-mockery.

"And I would never fill out a denim skirt and top like you do. We're like the three muses. We hit every facet." She winked at Vivian in the mirror as she finished brushing out her hair, wishing not for the first time it had some curl.

"Why aren't you ready?" Skye stood, leaning against the door frame. "I thought you'd meet us downstairs."

"And sure I would. If I knew you were coming over and wanted me to meet you."

She went back into her bedroom and circled around the bed to what was a surprisingly large walk-in closet. The idea of going to the parade had her wanting to step out of her typical summer dresses routine.

She grabbed a pair of linen shorts and a shell top and threw them on while listening to the girls bicker over lip gloss colors neither of them would ever wear. Checking herself in the mirror, she grabbed a sweater because the evening air was definitely going to get cooler.

"What was I supposed to be downstairs waiting for you for?" Lyra grabbed her little bag and pulled on a pair of Keds.

"Noah is having us over for a barbecue. I think he's trying to keep an eye on Spence and at the same time keeping him as amused as possible." Skye laughed at the idea, glad that didn't fall on her shoulders. "I'm also glad I didn't have to arrest him. Thanks for that."

"Day isn't over yet," Vivian added in.

"So we're all going to the barbecue and then the parade?"

Lyra tried to hide her disappointment, not to mention her annoyance, that her friends had decided to crash her maybe-date.

"Wow."

"What?" she asked as both her friends cracked up.

"Let's just say, I'm never taking you to Vegas." Vivian turned them all toward the door, hustling them like a mother hen with her little chicks. "Don't worry, we won't crash your date."

"Unless we have to," Skye added with her typical balance of overbearing responsibility and dry humor.

Instead of walking down to Noah's, they took Skye's jeep. She was always on call as the deputy sheriff during Christmas weekends, so wheels were a must.

It was dawning on Lyra just how much all of them put into the celebrations. Not that she was complaining, but she had never had anything she would rather do before.

They pulled up to Noah's and onto the gravel second driveway of his cottage. From the back of the house, they heard music and the deep rumble of male laughter.

Lyra was suddenly nervous. Not only was she going to have to deal with figuring out the situation between her and Spence, but she was going to have to do it with an audience.

An audience who believed in active participation.

A hand came down on her shoulder as she stood in the kitchen putting away the practice custards she'd messed up earlier that morning. Her friends wouldn't care what they looked like, only that they tasted good.

"Don't worry." Vivian gave her a reassuring smile while Skye marched to the back of the house. "I know I'm not the one to give the best romantic advice. Obviously that part of my life is on hold since I messed it up—"

"I don't think you could call getting pregnant as a teenager messing up your full romantic life." Lyra shook her head with a laugh.

Vivian never saw herself the way everyone else did. She was absolutely amazing and one of Lyra's heroes. Her mom did her best, but Vivian? Vivian did it all. Lyra was amazed at how awesome a mom she was.

"My point is, you do what's right for you. No matter what, you have us, and Starlight Harbor, and your bakery, and your family, and a boatload of other things I could keep listing. Taking the risk on one more thing is scary, and it might hurt, so I'm not going to downplay that. I respect you too much to blow daisies. I'm just saying your safety net will catch you if for some reason you fall."

Lyra felt her eyes tear up. Vivian wasn't one to share emotions very often, so when she did you had to listen because she was always speaking about nine levels deeper than most people even bothered to dig. Lyra reached out her hand. "I have the best friends in the world. "

"Darn straight you do." Vivian gave it a squeeze as she smiled and pushed Lyra toward the door. "Now go see what else you might have."

22

Spence

"So, man. You and Lyra?" Cam asked the question as he cut up potatoes at the kitchen counter and tossed them in a pot.

Spence had never watched anyone make potato salad from scratch, and here was Cam, practically doing it with his eyes shut.

He needed to up every game he had.

"Yeah?" Spence asked, because he didn't want to answer any questions he wasn't explicitly asked.

Cam grinned at Spence as he fished a colander out of the cabinet.

"I haven't exactly run the idea of me and Lyra by Lyra. But trust me, Cam, as soon as I do, I'll stop everything and call you."

Cam laughed, pointing the knife he was way too familiar with because of his day job at Spence and grinned. "I like you. Noah, he's afraid to like you. But I like you. Don't screw this up."

Spence hadn't even realized there was anything to screw

up until a couple hours ago. It felt like this whole town moved on a different time frame. Like Brigadoon, or something.

"Not screwing it up is only step one. I don't live here. I don't have a job here." Spence ran a hand through his hair, giving a slight tug before letting go. "In a few days, I might not have a job at all. "

"What about that magazine thing you run online that nearly destroyed Lyra?"

"I'm never going to live that down." Spence glanced out the window, letting his gaze travel over the last two rows of cottages and out to sea. "The truth is, I'm trying to sell it. Which is why I came here to begin with. To straighten this out to make sure I didn't lose my opportunity to dump that thing and make some much needed income off it."

Cam nodded. "Not like we didn't guess it was something like that." He turned to lean his hip against the counter, crossing his arms across his chest. "I assume it's not still like that?"

Spence shook his head. It was so far from like that now he didn't even know how he'd been standing in that spot just a couple days ago.

"Good." Cam seemed appeased by his simple answer. "That's all I really need to know. I leave that gossip crap to Jamie. He loves that stuff. Knows as much as Miss Angie about what goes on in this town."

Spence was about to ask about the older lady when the front door banged open.

"We're here," Skye announced as she strode into the room. "Lyra brought some custard thing. She says it looks like junk but tastes amazing."

Cam leaned down and kissed her on the cheek, which had her swatting at him with a bright grin.

"Lyra doesn't lie about desserts. I'll eat it if I have to do it blindfolded." Cam turned as the other two came in and gave a curt nod "Vivian."

Spence glance between the two of them, a little surprised at the tension since he'd never seen them together before.

Huh.

But his focus was dragged to Lyra, as if no one else in the room mattered one whit.

"Hey."

She gave him a shy smile that melted his heart even more. "Hey."

"Okay, enough with the googly eyes. Where's Noah?" Vivian glanced around as if his presence suddenly made itself known.

"Back deck, putting the steaks on." Spence frowned as Lyra gave him a small smile while Vivian herded her out.

He watched Cam watch Vivian with her long stride out of the kitchen and down the hall. He shook his head before he went back to his potato salad.

Looks like Spence wasn't the only one with a complicated situation.

He also wasn't above a wee bit of payback

"So, Vivian, huh?"

What he expected was a little light banter. Instead, he was taken by surprise when Cam braced his hands against the counter and dropped his head down in such a defeated stance Spence almost wasn't sure if he should hug him or call for help.

The moment was over before he could make a decision.

Cam straightened and turned back to look him in the eye. "It's not like that. And I guess maybe it never was."

He picked up a couple bowls and headed toward the back deck, obviously putting an end to the conversation.

Spence was going to have to remember no matter how welcome they made him feel, he was still an outsider and had to be more careful where he stepped. Especially with those he was coming to care for as friends.

23

Lyra

LYRA WAS SURPRISED HOW WELL SPENCE FIT IN WITH HER group.

She probably shouldn't have been. But it was just such a happy coincidence he got along with them that she didn't want to question.

The group hung out and ate and chatted and laughed. The sun dropped lower over the forest and mountains to the west, leaving its sunset trail of light to glimmer on the ocean before it disappeared. The food was great and the company better.

But the whole time Lyra was just waiting so she and Spence could head down to the parade.

A girl didn't put on her best maybe-date clothes to hang out with her friends.

When it was finally late enough for them to head out, Lyra pushed away from the table and stood.

"We have to get going. We don't want to be late and not have a spot on the green."

She glanced down at Spence, hoping he would take the

cue. The smart man was already stacking dishes to carry into Noah's on their way through.

"Great." Skye stood and grabbed a stack of trash as she did. "You guys can ride up with me. I have to be on call."

Lyra gave her friend a long stare, unsure if she was joking or really just that oblivious.

With Skye, it could easily be either one.

"Actually, Skye," Jamie jumped in. "I've been having some problems down on the water. Do you have a second?"

She glanced around as if unsure what she should do.

"It's okay." Lyra gave her a reassuring smile. "It's a nice night for a walk and Spence still hasn't seen the whole town."

"Oh. As long as it's okay." Skye was never sure what to do in social situations, so Lyra gave her a reassuring smile and all but pushed Spence through the door back.

Outside, they both glanced around as if surprised to finally find themselves alone.

"Dinner was nice."

"Really?" Lyra asked. Had he enjoyed himself or was he just being polite?

"Yeah. I like your friends. I appreciate how much they've done to make me feel comfortable."

That was exactly the right thing to say, she decided as she reached out and took his hand.

They walked up the hill to the green hand-in-hand, Lyra pointing out different things from her childhood. Skye's family home, the boy who took her to prom's house, the time she tried to rebel and went with Vivian to TP a certain guy's house.

Spence was fascinated by it all. It was like the entire world he'd been looking for his whole life was in a few square miles and he just now found it.

As they got up to the green, he was shocked to see the roads blocked off and the sidewalks packed.

"I hope we didn't wait too long. I don't want you to miss anything," he said, even though he was the guest.

"Don't worry. It's taken care of." She winked as she pulled him forward through the crowd and across the street, waving at the cop who rolled his eyes as Lyra carried on jaywalking when they were directed to walk around.

She just smiled and waved, tugging Spence behind her.

When they got to her shop, it was still closed, a sign on the door read SOLD OUT, OPEN TOMORROW with little cupcakes and hearts all over it.

Spence laughed as he looked at it and told her, "That's so you."

"Annoyingly girly?"

His hand gave hers a small squeeze.

"I was thinking more along the lines of super cute and considerate."

"Good answer."

But the best part was that the wrought iron bench that sat in front her shop with its matching chairs and tables had been pulled to the edge of the sidewalk and a large reserve sign placed on it.

"Skye called down to one of the deputies to make sure we had a spot, and since they dragged us to a barbecue, we might lose it."

"Your friends are above and beyond." He walked to the front of the bench where a little blanket sat resting on the cushions.

"Tell me what you think so far of Starlight Harbor."

Lyra expected him to say something blithe about the view or the people or even the cookies.

But instead, she found herself gazing into his dark brown eyes behind those black frames that were staring back at her with a strange intensity. And smiled. "I think my favorite part of Starlight Harbor is sitting right here."

If anyone else had said that to her, she would have told them it was the worst line in history. Instead, her heart started racing so fast she glanced down, afraid he could hear it.

"Oh."

She was saved from responding by the music entering at the far side of the square. It was so fun to see them coming in, the small band playing holiday tunes followed by marching elves tossing penny candy and toys. And then came the best part—okay, Lyra thought it was the best part.

Dancing reindeer.

The school dance corps handled this and every month the dance was different. There was a video collection of them on the private Facebook page the town had for locals only. She'd always loved watching their little antlered heads go by. But now she had a front row seat and got to see the entire routine when they reached her side of the square.

She was having so much fun, she was afraid she'd never want to leave the shop open again.

"This is great!" Spence shouted over the music. "Is it always this great?"

"Everyone says so. I really should figure out how to close up or maybe have a little cart out front instead so I can watch."

Either way, she was going to need to replace the twins for the rest of their high season.

The sleigh finished its way around the square and pulled to a stop. Santa hopped down and made his jolly way up to the gazebo, where his chair and elves awaited him so he could let all the children, and anyone else who wanted to, make a Christmas wish.

The crowd hurried over, leaving them sitting under the gas lanterns outside her shop.

"Maybe you should go make a wish," she teased, aware of how much he was enjoying himself.

"I don't have to." His gaze made her heart rush before his words. "You're right here."

24

Spence

SPENCE WAS PRETTY SURE HE WAS WAKING UP HAPPIER THAN HE ever had before in his life.

He'd been looking for something, he could see that now.

He would never have expected it would all be here in Starlight Harbor. Not just cupcakes, everything. The town, the friends he was making, the ability to write again, … And yes, Lyra.

He just needed to make it work.

He knew the guys had breakfast on Fridays at Noah's café, so he headed over. Jamie waved him over, sliding into the booth to let him join them.

"I'm glad we don't have to kill you." Jamie gave him a bright grin and dug back into his omelets.

"I'm kinda glad, too." Spence glanced at the menu board, trying to figure out what he wanted, when Noah walked over and slid an identical omelet under his nose with a link of sausages. "That looks great."

"Good. Because that's what you get. The father accidentally ordered the wrong thing and I have to feed it to someone." Noah walked away without adding anything.

It was still too early in the day for there to be a rush, and most of the people were staying at the inn where they could get breakfast.

"Who brings a notebook to lunch?" Jamie asked even as he continued eating.

"A man with a lot of decisions to make." Spence set the notebook aside and pulled the plate up. Decisions could wait.

Cam glanced at Jamie. "You are literally the only person at this table without a notebook. Maybe the better question is what kind of man comes to breakfast without a notebook."

Jamie took note of Cam's sketchbook, Spence's notebook, and Noah's work pad he carried around.

"Obviously a man who has a better memory than all his friends."

Cam shook his head and gave his attention back to Spence. "What kind of decisions?"

Spence would have thought he wasn't ready to talk about it yet. But, looking at the nonjudgmental gazes, he realized not only was he ready, but these men could have some good suggestions.

"It's fresh start time. I have to sell that albatross around my neck to get far enough out of debt to really be able to move on."

"And moving on involves Lyra?"

Spence nodded. He realized how stupid that sounded after a few days. It wasn't like he was buying a ring and carrying it around with him... Yet.

"I have a lot to do to get in a good place for her. One of those things, after selling the mess of a magazine I accidentally created, is to move here." He sipped the coffee Noah set out in front of him. "Basically, selling all my stuff should be no problem. That's what Craigslist is for. I don't need a lot, just enough to make a fresh start here. I know from what you guys have said people don't take a lot of risk on outsiders, but someone's got to be willing to rent me a place."

"Yeah, well." Jamie shook his head. "I wouldn't get your hopes too high. Most places someone might rent you long-term are booked through next year."

Noah gave him a long, steady look before nodding to himself as if he'd made a decision.

"I'll rent you the room."

All gazes shifted as one toward him, each with a different level of surprise.

"What?" Spence knew he couldn't have heard him correctly.

Noah shrugged as if it wasn't a big deal. "It's been fine the last couple days, and I could use the income to pay off the café quicker. Spence could figure out if he really wanted to move here. If Lyra kicks him out of town again…"

All the guys laughed.

You'd think two days was enough time to live down being kicked out of town by a five-foot-four baker. Apparently, not so much.

"Are you sure? Because that would be perfect."

Spence couldn't believe this, shocked and overwhelmed that not only did it seem like everything was coming together, but that he'd been accepted by this group of guys.

He definitely had to up his game.

Noah gave him a nod, as if it were all the same, not a big deal at all.

"Yeah, man. Definitely." Spence shook his head, too grateful to say more, but still, "I mean probably. The whole, getting run out of town thing by Lyra has to check out first."

Jamie laughed. "If the women folk could really run us out, only Noah would be left."

Noah shot him a gesture he couldn't get away with if there were guests present.

Spence finished his meal, listening to the banter among the friends and feeling more settled than he had in his adult life. He hadn't realized he'd been missing this.

It was an understated need for men—friendship.

How was it that everything a person, namely him, could need was all in this one small, magical quirky town?

Glancing at the clock, he knew it was the perfect time to see what Lyra thought. There was no reason to put it off.

He crossed the café, rounded the counter, and brought her right up to him in a kiss way too hot to be a good morning greeting, his heart going double time as she leaned into him, her hand coming up to wrap around his neck as if she wanted him there as badly as he wanted to be there.

Her small body fit against his unexpectedly perfect, and he couldn't help but think of another piece of his life clicking into place.

Finally easing away far enough to look down into her eyes, he couldn't help but grin like an idiot.

"What took you four years to answer that call for help I was obviously posting on my site every year?"

Lyra's hand slid around and cupped his cheek, something stronger than affection showing in her eyes. "I figured you'd smarten up. But, you just didn't."

"I needed a strong woman to straighten me out."

He kissed the tip of her nose because of those darn freckles and laughed when her caress turned into a swat.

Running the tips of her ponytail through his hands, he let the silk calm him as he prepared to take the first giant step in his new future.

"I just talked to Noah."

"Nice guy, that Noah." She went up on her toes and brushed her lips across his, distracting him completely with the light touch that grew more urgent as she leaned into him again.

A moment later, he was trying to remember what he'd wanted to say.

Oh, yeah.

"He said I could rent a room, move in with him."

She froze, leaning away and staring up at him with such a look of shock his heart dropped into his gut, then they both dropped into his shoes.

"You want to move here?"

"I was thinking I did."

"And live with Noah?"

"That seems to be the best option, seeing as it's the only one."

Lyra was quiet so long Spence was sure she wasn't happy with this idea.

"I don't want you to feel any pressure." He eased himself away, even as she grabbed onto his shirt, holding him in place. "I don't want you to feel like you need to humor me because I'm an absolute mess right now. But I'm getting better. I'm getting better for me, but I'll be my best for you."

She was shaking her head before he even finished the sentence.

"No, no. I should've said how exciting that was right away. I was just so surprised." She gazed up at him with suspiciously damp eyes. "I've been trying to brace myself for when you left. I hated the idea we might lose our chance before we even got it."

"Oh, thank goodness." He reached out and took her hand, giving it a squeeze. "The guys pointed out that if you kick me out of town again, it's easier to get out of renting a room from Noah than an actual lease, so there's absolutely no pressure. You know, except the pressure I'm going to put on with all the wooing."

"What will this wooing consist of?"

"There will be long walks out to the point, and lots of

Santa hats, and all the kisses you can put up with." He leaned down and demonstrated that last one. "But today's wooing consists of helping you get ready for tonight. I figured I could free you up to focus on the engagement party. Tomorrow will be soon enough to head back to my place and get things in order." He couldn't believe how amped up he was to be done with that part of his life.

And, he'd get out of debt no matter what. He'd figure it out. Write on the side, get a job. He could do it.

Even if he couldn't sell the site to anyone large enough to make a difference, maybe he could pass it off with some type of percentage deal.

None of it mattered—well, it did if he didn't want to meet the credit card's collections people. But he'd figure it out.

The weight of trying to jump from one life to another when neither of them was the right one for him lifted.

He glanced down at the woman in his arms. Sure, he said no pressure, but there was no way he'd let her go without giving her the best version of himself first.

Forget about upping his game. It was game on.

25

Lyra

LYRA SPENT THE REST OF THE MORNING MAKING SURE everything was good in the bakery before moving on to the finishing touches for the engagement party.

No matter how much work she had to do, she was floating around in little heart-shaped clouds.

If Vivian came in, the mockery level would probably shoot through the roof.

Every time Spence was done with something out front, he'd slide into the kitchen and steal kisses.

Not that she wouldn't have given them freely, but she liked how he'd surprised her in free moments.

He'd run across to Noah's to grab them lunch the first time one of her girls came in, giving her a little wink as he did and letting her have some time with Vivian.

In the quiet he left behind him, Lyra had her first moment of panic.

Not just *Oh, I'll get through this panic.* But the kind that had her leaning over, hands on her knees and trying to catch her breath.

What had she been thinking? Should a guy she'd only

known a few days move hours away from his home for a chance to get to know her?

Her?

This incredibly smart, sexy, ambitious guy was just going to drop everything and move to Starlight Harbor?

When Lyra saw Vivian through the door it was with a mixture of excitement and relief.

"After you give me those last two cranberry scones, you can tell me exactly what this whole look is that's going on with you." She waved her hand in front of Lyra as if to gesture at everything at once.

Since she had people in the store, Vivian came around to the little corner table Lyra kept squeezed between the door and the sink in the kitchen, seating herself with her scones and the most patient expression she could muster.

"Spence is selling his magazine and moving in with Noah."

She rushed through it, afraid it wasn't as exciting as she thought. Or that it was crazier than she thought it was.

"Huh. I think he and Noah will be very happy together."

Lyra reached over and took the plate of scones away.

"What am I supposed to do?" she demanded.

"Thank the universe you have more time to fall all the way and add those banana nut muffins back onto the menu?"

"Vivian, I'm serious."

"I am, too. Those banana nut muffins should not have come off the menu."

"If you're not serious, I'm going to call Skye. And we all know what happens when you try to have a non-literal conversation with her." Lyra crossed her arms over her chest, smearing the chocolate across her arm. "And I'll never put the banana muffins back on the menu."

Vivian gasped. "You wouldn't."

"Just watch me. I will blackmail you with those muffins in a heartbeat."

"Fine." Vivian set down the last half of the cranberry scone she had on the plate Lyra handed back to her. "Banana-nut-muffin-blackmail seriously, have you ever seen a man who needed a change more than Spence? I don't think it's just you he's moving for."

"Well, I would hope he was moving for himself, too. Otherwise that's just too much."

"Honey, I think it's more than that he's falling for you. I think he's found his second family here. The guys have taken him on even quicker than they dragged Noah into their circle. Skye and I like him and are just being wary in case we have to hide the body if he breaks your heart. Which, you know will go pretty smoothly, seeing as the deputy sheriff would be involved."

Vivian nodded to herself as if she were actually planning a murder in her head and Lyra was a little afraid to interrupt because you never knew with Vivian.

"And then," she continued, "there's Starlight Harbor. It heals people. And every once in a while, one of those people who it heals needs to come here and be part of it. Like how we got Noah. And I think your Spence is one of those. Not just because you're here, but because he realized he wanted something very different in life than what he had. And also because he's darn lucky you're here, too."

"Hello?" Spence called from the front as the door chime sounded. "Chicken salad on croissant...again."

He laughed as he made his way back to the kitchen. So what if she liked the same things every day?

Especially if he was one of those same things.

"Vivian, hey." He set down the bag on the table and gave her a grin. "Why don't you two eat that and I'll head back to Noah's. Jamie's trying to convince a woman from Ohio she should make him the next hero in her romance novel. She's currently asking him to model, which involves taking his shirt off and holding a broom like a claymore."

Lyra shook her head, laughing up at him. "And you gave that up to bring me a sandwich?"

"Darn tooting…but seriously. Vivian. Eat my sandwich. I'll be back." He rushed out the door before either of the women could stop him.

"Yeah. He's totally going to struggle fitting in here." Vivian opened the bag and pulled the sandwiches out.

"You just ate two scones."

"I wouldn't want to hurt his feelings."

Lyra glanced toward the front of the shop where Spence dodged around a slow-moving car on the opposite side of the street.

She took the step off the ledge and…let herself fall.

"Me neither."

L yra spent the rest of the day perfecting everything she needed to bring over to the inn for the party. Thank goodness Ms. Camilla would have everything set up on her end. That woman was a marvel.

With the kitchen prepped and everything ready to go out in shifts with servers to offer up to those mingling under the white fairy lights and Japanese lanterns, Lyra felt on top of the world.

"All right, Cupcake. That's the last of them." Spence gently set down the carrier with her cream tarts in it. "That van is amazing."

"Craigslist. A baker had thought he'd blow up overnight in Portland and bought everything a famous pastry chef might need. Three months later, he started Craigslisting things. I lucked out. That new oven? Also him."

"Wow, that's tough." Spence grimaced before he could flash her a smile. "But lucky for you."

It was surprising how well they worked together. She was already trying to figure out how to make Spence take a paycheck. He'd not only been everywhere she'd needed him, but he'd known instinctively this was different than the shop for her.

This was more of a show. More of a presentation.

It wasn't welcoming people into her kitchen and feeding them.

It was part of a grand affair.

He kept her calm and centered, letting her know everyone outside was enjoying the mini-desserts and letting her focus on assembling and frosting the last parts of the cake as he dealt with any issues.

It was like they'd been doing this for years.

"I'll load this on a tray for Ms. Camilla's niece, then we're good to go. They have the toast and then dinner."

Thank goodness for outside caterers.

"I saved you a lemon tart." He slid her a treat wrapped in a napkin. "I know you keep your sugar count low, but you deserve it."

She couldn't believe he noticed she always went for the lemon…or that she avoided eating her own creations regularly.

"Thanks." She hopped up on the barstool at the counter. "Wow, this is good. Someone really talented must have made it."

Spence leaned in and kissed her. "Yup, lemony."

"Do you think—"

Spence rolled his eyes as his cell rang. "Hold that thought."

He strode across the kitchen in his no-nonsense way and grabbed the phone.

His head swung toward her, alert and excited.

"It's a potential buyer."

Lyra rushed over and looked down at it, the name lit up so well known even she was familiar with it.

He closed his eyes and pushed out a breath. "I need this whole part of my life behind me so badly."

"You answer that. I'm going to run to the restroom." She went up on her toes and kissed him on the cheek. "Good luck."

She hurried up to the guest floor where the restrooms were. She couldn't believe it. He'd said he doubted he'd get a call at all. Probably just an email saying they didn't value his site at anything they'd spend the money he was asking for.

And there it was. On a Friday night.

These guys needed to get a life.

She hurried through washing her hands and heading back downstairs, hoping he had good news already.

"No. The new exposé is non-negotiable." Spence's voice carried through the hall to the stairway as she made her way down.

There was a long pause and then he went on, "It's not just righting a wrong. It's a great piece. The article would be a bit off from what's been posted lately, but an occasional in-depth article would only create a feeling of a special exposé, something more interesting instead of less—Right. I understand, but—Did you see the other thing I sent you yesterday?"

Lyra wasn't sure if she should go into the kitchen or wait in the sitting room across the hall. Either way, she'd be listening, but would it ruin his flow if she walked in? She didn't want to put him off his game, so she dropped onto the sofa to wait. He knew she was coming right back, so it wasn't like she was eavesdropping.

"I get it. Yeah. You can't publish it, but you're okay with everything else?"

Lyra froze. He wasn't going to publish it? After all this, he was going to sell the site and not make things right first?

"Great," Spence went on from the other room. "I'll be back in New York tomorrow. I can get everything ready with my lawyer and we'll go from there."

She sat there, trying to pull it together. How could he do this? After all he'd done to make things right with her, with her business, with her town, he was just going to throw it all away?

She'd been so stupid. WWVD was all about risks and she'd taken one and look where it got her.

Lyra took a deep breath and headed into the kitchen, realizing this was not the place to have it out with him since she had this gig to finish.

Clearing her mind of everything she wanted to say, she pasted on a smile and strode in, hoping he'd tell her exactly what he'd done.

"Hey!" He tossed the phone down and came toward her, picking her up and spinning her around. "They're buying the site. I can't believe I'll be free of it finally."

She forced a smile on her face, and he was too excited about it if anything was off. "That's great. And everything went as you hoped?"

"It's a little different than I wanted, but it'll do." He leaned down to kiss her, and she turned to give him her cheek. "But yeah, I have to go home and deal with the lawyers. And then I'm free."

Lyra couldn't believe what she was hearing. Did he really think that once she found out about the article, everything would be fine?

"Any surprises?" she asked, hoping he'd come clean, hoping this would be the moment that he showed her that he was the person he said he was going to be.

No more singing sharks.

"Not really. Nothing I didn't plan for."

Her whole body flashed hot and cold. She wasn't sure she could feel the tips of her fingers. Reaching out, she brushed them across the table, wondering if the counter was that cold or her fingertips were freezing.

"Nothing?"

Spence shook his head. Looking pretty proud of himself actually. "Nope. It's good to go."

Lyra stepped away, holding up her hand to stop him when Spence came toward her.

"Really? And things are good for my shop?"

Spence nodded, looking confused and maybe a little annoyed. "Yeah."

"I think you should go."

Spence froze looking at her in shock. "What?"

"Do you really think I'd want to be with someone who could do these things to me? Who hurt me and my town like this?"

"I thought we moved past that. I'm not that guy anymore. I'm not sure I ever was."

"Oh, I'm sure. You just proved that." Lyra rounded the kitchen counter, putting it between them. "You should leave and don't come back. And I need you to do that right now, because I have to get this cake finished and out there so that those wonderful people can celebrate what they have. Honesty, loyalty, and love. If you ever figure out any of those things... You know what? No. Don't bother."

With that, she rolled the cake toward the catering door, leaving him standing there watching her go.

He was gone when she got back.

Spence

Spence headed back to Noah's completely at a loss. He wasn't sure what he could do right now. He didn't want to ruin her big event, so leaving when she asked him to was the best plan.

But he was coming back. Absolutely.

Noah was out with Jamie fishing—a pastime he claimed bored him to tears but that he had all the gear for.

The relief Spence felt not having to tell the guys that he'd somehow gotten back on the wrong foot again with Lyra was immense.

Plus, he didn't want Noah to have an opportunity to tell him he wasn't welcome.

Grabbing the overnight and laptop bags he'd arrived with, he hit the road.

The drive home was quick. He was so focused on getting things done, he spent most of it on the phone organizing as fast a turn around as he could until everyone went to bed and it was just him and the truckers.

It was shocking, now that his parents had moved to Florida, really how little there was to do or keep. Since Noah's place was furnished, Spence spent an hour putting almost all his belongings on Craigslist, clearing out so much junk he was shocked.

As soon as he could, he cut his lease, packed his must-haves, clothes, and equipment and computers in a small U-Haul and headed back to Maine, excited to get back home.

Home.

He'd been gone just over a week and all he could think was, "How did I live like this? Without sunshine and forever?"

He left Noah a message he'd be back that evening and hit the road, more than happy to pay the thirty-day notice on his lease to get out of it. He hadn't realized how stressed he'd become until his shoulders relaxed when he hit the Maine border.

It was nearly eleven when he parked in front of the cottage he'd be calling home for a while. Noah was probably passed out already with the hours he kept for the café, so Spence grabbed his essentials and headed in, ready to crash for the night.

He'd quietly opened the door, only to find Noah sitting in the front room, nursing a beer over a Blake Banner book.

"Hey." Spence set the bag down and studied Noah, getting the vibe very quickly that all was not well in Starlight Harbor. He dropped into the other overstuffed leather chair and leaned forward. "Okay, give it to me straight."

"Weren't going to get it any other way." Noah studied him a long moment, more inscrutable than usual. "How'd you leave things with Lyra?"

"Less than great," Spence admitted.

"Yeah, you might want to downgrade that."

Spence's excitement at being home dimmed. "By how much?"

Noah glanced away before taking a deep breath and meeting Spence head on. "All the way."

Spence collapsed back in his seat, shocked it had come to is. If he'd known, he would have stayed, not given her the week to get angrier, to settle into her decision.

He wasn't even sure how she had gotten there.

She knew he'd have to go home to finish the deal, to make a clean break.

"Here's the deal. I think you screwed up again, but maybe not how she thinks. Maybe it's one of those small screw ups all guys make where we assume we can talk about something later and then it snowballs." Noah kept going, more words than Spence had heard from him together at once. "If that's what's going on, then stick around. Fight for her. Figure it out. If it's not, then I'd say lay low and figure out how to get through this. I offered you a place as a friend. It's yours. But, if you've done something unforgivable, remember, I won't forget."

"Don't tell her I'm back. I need twenty-four hours to put my plan in place. It's been getting set up all week."

Noah sat, silent and unreadable before finally agreeing. Once he had, he got up and went to bed without another word.

Spence knew this was his only chance to win her back. He wasn't going to be like her family—there but not.

He was going to be the family she deserved.

Lyra

LYRA'S STOMACH HAD ACHED ALL WEEK, AS IF SHE'D EATEN four pounds of fudge, then gone for a run. Which, why would anyone do that to themselves?

The run, not the fudge.

Skye did it all the time and she wasn't dead.

Yet.

But she was pretty sure that's what this must feel like.

If this was what heartbreak felt like, she was glad it wasn't catchy.

Vivian and Skye had been even more supportive, if that was possible. Vivian saying that if he came back and didn't bring the Golden Apple as an apology gift, she'd take care of him.

Skye was pragmatic, and while that was good, Lyra wasn't ready to hear most of her thoughts yet.

So, when the bell over the shop door chimed before she was open, she was pretty sure it was a heart-check by one of her friends before they went to work.

"I told you. I'm fine. Stop checking up on me." She shouted while she focused on her newest invention.

Lemon peanut butter cups.

So far, they weren't coming out right. But as a woman who was renouncing men and also cats because she was allergic to them, she had plenty of time in her future.

"The thing is..." She froze at the voice, wanting it to go away, because how dare he? How *dare* he? "I'm not. I'm not fine at all."

She braced, waiting for him to come into her kitchen and emotionally overwhelm her space. But instead, he didn't. He waited, on the other side of the counter where he should be.

She brushed her hands off, floury bits of peanut butter flaking off them, and stared, wishing she'd brought something heavy to throw at him.

"That's a shame. Had a rough week? Didn't take down any small businesses lately?"

"No. Worse. I thought I was falling in love with this girl—and I was—but she wasn't falling in love with me."

"Oh! How dare you! Don't you accuse me of not falling in love with you! You sold me out."

"Did I?" Spence sounded completely surprised by that. As if he didn't know what he did.

"Yes! You told them they didn't have to correct the issue with the Tiny Tacky Town and make things right with my business."

Spence froze and crossed his arms in a defensive move. "And you thought that meant I'd sold you out?"

How could she believe he thought that was okay?

"Yes. Absolutely. You went back on your promise."

"And you know this because you asked me. You said, *Spence, I overheard something that didn't make sense and figured I'd ask you what happened?* Because I don't remember that conversation, so that might be why I'm so confused." The sarcasm was so thick she thought even Skye would spot it.

But sarcasm wasn't a defense. It was deflection.

"It was pretty clear."

Spence stepped back, his eyes narrowed and jaw tight. "You know what, Cupcake? Maybe before you throw someone away, you check to make sure they're really garbage first."

He turned and stormed out of her shop, leaving her completely confused about what just happened.

He'd broken her heart. What did he have to be angry about?

Well, if he was sticking around, he'd see the answer was nothing.

As in, he'd get nothing from her—he wouldn't see her hurting. He couldn't win her back even if he figured out how to make peanut butter lemon cups work.

"You," Vivian pointed at her over the crumble cake she was devouring, "are out of control."

Lyra froze elbow deep in dough, a little put out that Vivian was complaining while she ate crumble cake happily. She glanced at Skye for backup.

"Don't look at me. I'm not the one having a sale because I'm baking seventeen hours a day and not sleeping." She bit into the asiago bun. "By the way, this new recipe is fabulous."

She wasn't sure how much of their *support* she could take. One of them seemed to be with her at all times and they were beginning to wear on one another.

"I have a right to be angry. He betrayed me."

"Okay, drama queen. Let's slow down a bit. He had a point with the whole not asking him. And, I've got a friend monitoring his site. The sale went through a couple days ago, your post is still hidden, and nothing new has gone live. It's not much of a betrayal."

"But he kept promising he'd fix it. That was not fixing it."

"Honey." Vivian put her cake down, so Lyra knew she was serious. "Neither of you talking to one another isn't going to fix this either."

"Who says I want to fix it?" She hadn't. She'd tossed him out and yet no one had run him out of town or needed to hide the body.

Noah was still offering him sanctuary.

"Thought bubbles," Vivian said, making a show of reading the blank space above her head.

"It's just, I took the plunge." She tried to hold back the tears. "And I hit the rocks at the bottom of the cliff. My mom finally got back from wherever the heck she'd been and told me, *well, Lyra, broken hearts make the best artists*, picked up a tart, and flounced out."

"Why in the world were you asking your mother for advice?" Skye looked at her like she was nuts.

Maybe she was.

"It's just—"

The front door chimed and Vivian glanced out the kitchen door. "Speak of the devil."

"Lyra, darling. I'm so glad you got everything straightened out. Those Google alerts were so much better than the last ones. That new site is lovely. Absolutely lovely. And it looks like the writer is even off on a new adventure already. He's at a small former shaker village over in New Hampshire, teasing the next exposé. Very exciting." She patted her daughter on the cheek and took a cookie. "See? Your stars have realigned and everything worked out for the best. Bye, girls."

The door fell shut behind her and silence reigned.

"Hurricane Linda." Skye shook her head as Lyra pulled out her tablet.

"What do you think that meant?"

It took exactly one second to find.

THE BACKYARD TOURIST
    Starlight Harbor, Maine
    A town filled with Everyday Magic
    #LoveHappensHere
    by Spence Côte

"Oh." Lyra rushed through the article amazed what he'd done. It was a brand new site focused on local travel, seeing your own backyard, enjoying short, affordable vacations, and even the occasional splurge.

The entire thing was already set up with announcements for each of the Starlight Harbor pieces.

The first one was an introduction, posted yesterday. The second was about her bakery, raving about her food and then going on a personal bend.

> "If you're lucky, you'll get to meet the baker. Lyra Grigor is as sweet as her treats. Her heart goes into everything with full abandon, rushing in with a bravery that shows in her work.
>
> "I can't recommend her shop highly enough.
>
> "Although, I should give a disclaimer. I fell even more in love with Lyra than I did with her sugar cookies."

There was another paragraph wrapping it up with her bakery's info and then a link to his newsletter. Along the sidebar was an Instagram feed, a picture of Spence at the farm he was touring, pounding on a hot piece of metal in a blacksmith's shop.

"What do I do?" Lyra couldn't think, couldn't focus. "He was right. I should have asked."

"Yes, well, he should have told you. You're both idiots."

"Thank you, Skye."

She shrugged. "Well, he's been moping around all week at Noah's and now he's back moping again instead of coming over here and talking to you—"

"Wait, he's back? I thought he was in New Hampshire."

"He was, but that's all of what, three, four hours? It's not like it's Idaho."

Lyra pulled her apron off and tossed it at Skye as she passed. "Lock the door and put the sign up when you're done. Vivian, stay away from the banana nut muffins."

She had a man to win back.

Spence

Two more articles scheduled.

He was exhausted, but he needed to get ahead of the curve. He hadn't expected to have to go live so soon, but obviously things changed. The group who bought his site wanted it ASAP. That meant he needed to have his new income and his promise to Lyra fulfilled with The Backyard Tourist as soon as possible.

If he could get the next two weeks in order, he could get back to focusing on his life and see if what he thought he and Lyra had was real.

He shook his head.

He *knew* how he felt. He'd thought it was too soon, that he could soft step into love. He was an idiot.

Of course, that had been decided upon and confirmed over and over again this month.

But, he didn't know if she felt the same way. He was willing to risk it though, because she was the forever out on the horizon.

Nearly done with the next article, he jumped when the front door slammed open.

"Where is he?" Lyra's voice demanded.

Noah mumbled something, which was obviously him selling Spence out because her tiny, rapid footsteps were coming his way.

Standing up, he faced the door, waiting for her, waiting for the anger and accusations again.

He was ready, ready to love her through all of that.

"You jerk." Lyra came rushing in the room, all pink cheeks and bright freckles. "You absolute jerk. I've been broken-hearted in agony and you could have ended that. Could have told me that you were fixing it. That you weren't a promise breaker."

Spence wasn't sure what to say.

He zoomed in on the one thing that mattered—*broken-hearted*.

She loved him, too.

"What are you grinning at, you lying promise keeper?" she demanded.

"That you love me."

"So what if I did?"

"Do. You love me." He rocked back on his heels, happy to be in her line of fire. "If you didn't, you wouldn't be so mad."

"I'm really, *really* mad."

"That's okay, because I really, really love you, too."

She sighed, a completely exasperated sound.

"Spence, you should have told me. You just left, walked out. I thought you weren't coming back. Even when I thought I hated you, I needed you to come back. I needed to depend on that. People keep leaving and coming back or not coming back and I never know when or if."

"I will always, always come back, Cupcake."

"My family isn't the best at promises."

"So I've gathered. But I will be." He came and took her in his arms. "But, Lyra, you have to fight for us, too. I left because I didn't want to disrupt your job at the party. You made it bigger than it needed to be because you wouldn't talk to me."

"I hate talking."

Spence laughed, "You absolutely do not hate talking. But, I'd rather do this right now."

He leaned down, brushing his lips across hers as if for permission and felt his heart nearly explode with happiness when she sighed and leaned in to his kiss.

It was exactly what he'd always wanted.

Starlight Harbor was the place he lived.

Lyra was home.

EPILOGUE

CAM CARRIED YET ANOTHER BOX THROUGH NOAH'S HOUSE TO the back bedroom. For a guy who insisted he'd be traveling light, Spence had a lot of crap.

"Don't put that there." Vivian pointed back toward the hall. "It clearly says BATHROOM on it."

"I can read. I just thought we could put all the boxes in one place and let Spence sort them when he wanted."

"Yes. And if by 'sort them' you mean do the extra work of putting them in the right room, great."

"Fine." Cam picked the box back up. "We're just going to move him in a few months anyway, when he and Lyra get their love life in line."

She pointed at the box and then at the bathroom.

Fine. He'd carry the box up Mount Washington if she wanted.

Vivian was in rare form today. He was used to being on the receiving end of that temper, but today seemed especially bad.

It was like...a looking glass.

Both of them carrying boxes into a cute little house, unpacking it together, seeing what might have been.

She turned and caught him watching her, her shoulders stiffening as she pivoted and strode out of the house.

Vi could hold a grudge like no one else on Earth, but if there was one thing he'd learned from Spence winning Lyra over, it was this:

Even a Santa-hat-wearing idiot could win the love of his life back.

Cam grinned. It was time to get to the wooing.

ALSO BY BRIA QUINLAN

STARLIGHT HARBOR Series

The Sweetest Things

Book 2 - Cam & Vivian's Story

BREW HA HA Series

It's In His Kiss (FREE Prequel)

The Last Single Girl

Worth the Fall

The Catching Kind

The Proposing Kind

Things That Shine - A Crossover Brew Ha Ha /Double Blind Story

Bria's YA set RVHS Secrets

Secret Girlfriend

Secret Life

And YA Standalone

Wreckless

ABOUT BRIA

Quirky Girl and all around lovable klutz, Bria Quinlan writes Diet-Coke-Snort-Worthy Rom Coms about what it's like to be a girl and deal with crap and still look for love.

She also writes books for teens that take hard topics and make you laugh through your tears…or maybe cry through your laughter. Some people call them issue books. Some people call them romantic comedies. Bria calls them what-life-looks-like.

Her stories remind you that life is an adventure not to be ignored.

If these things are important to you: she's a RWA RITA, Golden Heart, & Cyblis nominee as well as a USA Today Best Seller, and natural blonde represented by the awesomely amazing Laird Lauren Macleod of the Clan…. Oh, wait. Of Strothman Agency.

Want to hangout? Check her out here:
briaquinlan.com/

Made in United States
North Haven, CT
01 February 2023

31936748R00107